I0684581

Hector and Steele

New Mexico Stories Book 2

By
A.C. Katt

Copyright © 2016 by A.C. Katt
ISBN: 978-1-68361-052-6
Cover art by Tibbs Designs

Published by Decadent Publishing Company, LLC
Look for us online at:
www.decadentpublishing.com

Chapter One

Monday, After Midnight

Sheriff Hector Gomez's shaft felt as if someone had encased it in warm, wet velvet. He lifted his head and gazed down the length of the bed. He wasn't dreaming. Perched above his thighs, his sometime lover had him in his hot mouth. Steele Adams, the Special Agent in Charge of the Albuquerque Office of the FBI, with sleep-tousled hair and languorous blue eyes, stared at him from the bottom of the bed. Adams' lips curled over the soft head of Hector's cock. He moved his mouth from Hector's shaft and opened the nightstand, getting out the lube to prepare him for entry. Steele rolled on a condom and slipped inside Hector's channel.

The only sounds in the room were Hector's moans and the slap of Steele's balls on his ass. Steele put his hand between them and began to move it up and down the sheriff's cock. His full ass tightened. He felt his balls draw up and the clenching of his walls, could almost feel Steele fill him through the latex. He spilled over his lover's hand. Steele pulled out and padded to the bathroom. The last thing Hector remembered was a cloth gently washing his stomach and genitals, and Adams whispering something in his ear.

Tuesday, Early Morning Mid-November

Hector woke and reached out. The space beside him felt cold and empty, as it did every morning. He must have fallen asleep last night, and Steele, as usual, went back to his own bed. Hector was heartily sick of their *friends with benefits* arrangement. Feelings had never been discussed between them; they had fallen into bed with one another a month after the FBI agent moved into the house. Hector wanted to change the parameters of their relationship or end it. He had fallen for Steele, hard, and the way things stood now, his love life served as an exercise in frustration.

Hector got up and went into the attached bath. Willing his bad mood away, he let the shower beat down hard on his body. Dressing in a newly dry-cleaned uniform, he went downstairs to the kitchen. Steele had left fresh coffee and some blueberry muffins. He must have been up early because they were homemade not store-bought.

He poured a cup of coffee into the travel mug he used in the Sheriff's Department Explorer and wrapped a muffin in a napkin. He had no time to attempt to unravel the mysteries of Steele's mind this morning; the department had an equipment check, and he had to oversee the inventory.

Tuesday, Late Afternoon

Hector Gomez answered what he thought to be a domestic violence call. The neighbor who called it in sounded hysterical. As the Sheriff of Sandoval County, he took too many calls for domestic abuse. They usually involved alcohol or drugs but something in his cop's gut told him this was different. He pulled into the driveway, got out of his Explorer, and saw a wild, glassy-eyed man standing on the rock-strewn lawn, waving a gun, and beating a ten-year-old kid about his body. The man wasn't drunk, he was high. He had the kid on the ground, kicking him in the ribs, groin, and legs with steel-toed boots. The gun waved threateningly in the child's face, which the kid tried to protect with waif-thin arms.

The man and the youngster appeared to be of Hispanic origin. The boy had rolled up in a ball in the front of the house, clothed in nothing but holey blue jeans and a thin T-shirt. Although only mid-November, New Mexico was experiencing an early cold snap due to the enormous El Nino build-up in the Pacific. He jumped from his Explorer and quickly shouted at the man to step away.

"I'm going to kill you, you little faggot." He pulled the trigger as the boy tried to roll away. He fired the gun a second time, barely missing the boy.

Gomez's backup, Deputy Edwards, fired a warning shot. The man turned to Edwards and pointed the gun. Hector shot the weapon out of his hand. The man fell next to the boy and spit in the kid's face. After Edwards helped him separate the man from the boy, Hector instructed him to call a bus and the Children, Youth, and Families Department

"Take him to UNM Sandoval. After the medics are through with him, book him and hold him for arraignment on attempted murder, child abuse, child endangerment, resisting arrest, and anything else you can think of to throw at him."

While waiting for the second bus so the EMTs could take the kid to the hospital, he got a blanket from his trunk and draped it around the boy whose chest heaved with sobs.

"What's your name, son?" Hector knelt and put his arm around the boy's shoulders.

"Matteo. Matteo Pena."

A woman at the storm door shouted obscenities in Spanish, prominently featuring the word *maricón*, a derogatory term for gay.

Suddenly, a small boy of about five came barreling out of the house and threw himself onto the older boy. "What did he do to you? Are you okay? You can't leave. You can't leave me alone with them." He sobbed as he held on tight to his brother.

"I demand that you let me take my younger son back into the house. Felipe, come." She grabbed the kicking and screaming child, gave him a casual slap, and dragged him back through the door.

"Matteo, Matteo, please. You can't leave me here."

The brother, clearly fearful and still sobbing, raised his face to Hector. "What do I do? She'll take this out on Felipe, and he isn't strong enough to handle her or him."

Hector put his arm around the kid's shoulder again. "Your father, such as he is, will be in the county lockup, at least for the night. We can figure things out in the morning. I won't let him hurt your brother."

4

"But she will. She isn't as strong as him, but she'll use the belt to hurt Felipe for coming out of the house." The boy's chest heaved as tears ran down his cheeks unchecked. "Why was I so stupid? Now Felipe is going to get punished, and it's my fault. They weren't supposed to be home."

The kid turned his head toward the little boy still crying at the door. "Felipe, don't get into trouble. I'll come get you. I won't leave you alone for long."

The woman slapped the younger child a second time. The sheriff planned to call CYFD as soon as he made it into the squad car. The smaller boy began to wail.

When the mother finally ran out of obscenities, she spat on the ground. "I don't want him here making my younger son into a pervert. You take him and don't bring him back," she hissed at Hector.

"Matteo...you can't leave," the younger boy cried.

He raised his eyes to Hector; hopelessness lay dull on his pupils.

Hector ignored the woman he presumed to be the mother and quietly asked the boy what happened. The boy seemed hesitant to answer, head spinning around seemingly to find an escape route, then back at his brother who still called his name despite the mother's efforts to stop him.

Hector squeezed his shoulder. "It's all right, son. I'm gay, too."

The boy puffed out a sigh of relief. "Papi found me searching for pictures of guys online. I know I'm gay. I've known since I was really little. I didn't tell them. I knew how it would be. They were supposed to be out until late tonight. It's the first time I surfed the net to see men online. I wanted to see articles on gay men, not porn." The kid's face screwed up in disgust.

"I've started to grow hair. I wanted to know if that's normal or is it so early because I'm gay. I couldn't ask him.

"He threw me out front and started beating on me then pulled the gun. I knew he didn't like *maricónes*, but I'm his son. He's supposed to love me." The boy pulled the blanket around his shoulders, tears still rolling down his cheeks. "I'm worried about my brother. I protect him from them. He's going to be all alone." The boy shook.

"Family should matter, but sometimes it doesn't. Let's get you examined by the docs. It will come out okay, I promise. I'll see what I can do about your brother. Here are the medics. They'll check you out. After that, I'll find you a place to stay for the night."

Hector followed the boy to the hospital, calling Children Youth and Families to meet him in the ER. The other bus preceded them, taking the father. At UNM Sandoval, the sheriff found his friend Aden Shaeffer-Rourke manning the ER desk. "What are you doing here? Aren't you an OR nurse?"

"I'm recently certified in ER Medicine, and they called Dare in to do a complicated emergency heart surgery. I'm not on the surgical rotation today, but Torres asked me to pull a shift in the ER. With Dare busy upstairs, I didn't have a reason to say no. Tomorrow is our day off. Who's the boy?"

"A gay kid, a victim of his father's machismo. Concerned that he grew pubic hair, he looked to find gay men online so he could compare his privates. The father came home and caught the boy browsing and threw him out on the rocks in front of the house. He kicked him in the ribs, head, and groin. He tried to shoot the kid twice. One of the neighbors called our office. He pulled a gun on Edwards."

"Bastard." Aden spat out the word. "He's just a kid." He glanced toward the ER cubicle where they'd brought the boy. "I'm charge nurse here tonight. I'll make sure they take good care of him. Did you call CYFD?"

"They're on their way. I'm planning on waiting here to meet the social worker. Matteo is worried about his brother. Watching the parents, I think he has reason to be." Hector took off his hat and turned it in his hands. "That could have been me. My papi became angry when I told him about me, but he didn't throw me out of the family. He's an old man now, but he's adjusted to what I am. He doesn't approve, but he tolerates my presence."

"I'll check on the kid and tell you what the doctor says. You'll need that for the incident report. Where is the mother?" Aden shuffled through some papers.

"She spat on the ground and told us not to bring the kid back. She didn't want him. He needs a foster home, but that may not be so easy because he's gay and an adolescent. I'm thinking of calling Steele and seeing if we can take him in. I qualified as a foster parent last year but specified I would only take gay kids."

Aden sighed. "My mother threw me out eight years ago, but she didn't try to beat the life out of me. I'm grateful Mom mellowed. She's still trying to make it up to me. Sometimes she's over the top about it. Speaking of Steele, how are things between the two of you? He's been living with you for almost six months. Is he even trying to find his own place?"

Hector frowned. "We're circling each other like wary cats. We fuck, but, immediately afterward, he goes to his bed or I go to mine. Neither one of us wants to admit we could be emotionally involved."

"A Mexican standoff, so to speak." Aden chuckled.

"He hasn't made any move to find his own place. I think both of us have been badly burned before and that makes you careful." Hector frowned.

"Careful is two to three months. This is ridiculous. You've been living in the same house for almost six months. You should have at least talked by now. Are you even gay?" Aden's expression was quizzical. "We're supposed to be able to communicate with each other."

"We've gone out to dinner a few times, but, so far, everything has been strictly physical." Hector changed the subject. "Could you check on the boy? I see Beatrice Marks bustling down the corridor. She's probably here about Matteo."

Aden took the chart and went in to see the kid. He grimaced. The boy had definitely taken a severe beating. His face had been largely spared except for a huge bruise on his cheek, but his chest, legs, and scrotum were a mess. The doctor had ordered X-rays, and the kid had been put on watch for a concussion. Matteo had deep-chocolate eyes and creamy tanned skin. He would be a stunner when he was older. What would Steele say when Hector told him he was bringing the kid home?

Aden took Matteo's vitals. "You still awake? If you're hurting, I can get you something for the pain."

"No, I'm okay." He was lying because, every time he moved, he winced.

"You don't get much rest in the hospital. People are always coming in to adjust your IV and check the machines. You're due to go down to X-ray soon. With all the moving around, you should take the pill. Don't worry, nothing will happen to you. I'm a friend of Hector, the sheriff. My name is Aden. I'll take good care of you." He handed Matteo the pill and some water. The kid put the pill in his mouth, took the water, and swallowed. Aden took the cup back and set it on the nightstand.

"Are you gay, too...his boyfriend or something?" Matteo whispered.

"Is it that obvious I'm gay?" Aden laughed. "No, I'm not Hector's boyfriend. I'm married to a cardiothoracic surgeon who works here at the hospital, Dare Rourke."

"A gay doctor. Why did he say I'd amount to nothing because of the way I am? Why can't he see I'm the same kid, even though I'm gay? I'm no different than my brother. I just like boys." Tears poured down his face in rivulets.

"Some people just refuse to confront their prejudice with facts and embrace change."

"Papi is one of those. The only change he embraces is a change in the way he cooks his meth." The kid appeared disgusted. Aden heard what he said about meth and made a note on the chart.

Matteo had the idea pounded into the head, from both of his parents, all of his life, that gay people were useless poufs. But, how could a pouf do the jobs the sheriff, this nurse, and his husband, the heart surgeon did? His parents were wrong.

He shouldn't be ashamed of what he was. Gay people could make it in the world. They could do well. He lifted his head toward the nurse. "Where am I?"

"UNM, Sandoval." The nurse read his electronic chart. "Depending on the result of the X-rays, and providing you don't have a concussion, you're in pretty good shape."

"What about my privates? He kicked me down there." Matteo felt his face warm up.

"The chart says you've urinated and there was no blood. I think you're going to be sore for a while from the trauma of the beating, but your privates should be in working order." Aden's eyes seemed to sparkle as Matteo breathed a sigh of relief.

The chart dinged. The nurse made a few notes on the electronic pad. "I'll have the doctor come in and talk to you as soon as we get the results of your X-rays." He left the room.

Fifteen minutes after Aden brought him back to the cubicle, a man came into the room wearing big black glasses, with dark hair, brown eyes, and green scrubs. "I'm Doctor Fernandez." He spoke briskly. "You're pretty banged up, but you managed to protect your face. You're going to have a livid bruise on your cheek, but the bone isn't broken. He managed to crack a few of your ribs and bruise your scrotum, but cracked ribs heal and your privates are safe." Fernandez chuckled. Matteo sent a mental *thank you* to Jesus.

"I'm only worried about a slight concussion because the pupils of your eyes are blown, so I'm going to keep you here for the rest of the night to check on that. Let someone know immediately if you're nauseous, get a headache, if you get dizzy, or start seeing flashes of light. Do you remember if you blacked out?"

"I didn't. I felt every kick and remember exactly what he said." Matteo rubbed his bruised arms.

"Well, at least there is no lasting damage to your body," Hernandez said thoughtfully. "Your mind is something else. You need someone to talk to?"

Matteo shrugged. "Where am I going to go?" Realization of his situation made him involuntarily drop his jaw. "I have nowhere to live and no clothes, nothing." He began to sniffle.

"I'll talk to Sherriff Gomez and see if the social worker has arrived." The doctor was exiting the room as Matteo realized how desperate his situation was. *Who is going to take in a gay kid with nothing?*

***

Hector met Beatrice Marks at the door of the emergency room. After giving her a brief rundown of the situation, Hector watched Beatrice shake her head.

"You're not going to be able to place him with a family, are you?" he asked.

"You're right. Gay kids are difficult, if not impossible, to place anywhere but a group home, and that isn't a good solution, either. In group homes, the gay kids are generally abused by the others, and the staff either doesn't know or refuses to see it. Being gay is particularly difficult if you're Hispanic."

Hector said dryly, "I know."

That brought her head up. "Oh, I didn't remember that you're gay." Beatrice blushed.

"I'd like to take him. My roommate and I live in Rio Rancho, so he won't have to change school districts," Hector said. "I own my home, and I'm already qualified to be a foster parent. Can you make an emergency placement for Matteo with me and work to make it permanent? My partner will take the parenting classes and do whatever it takes for him to be certified, too. If he won't, I'll take him alone."

"I'm sure I can get permission for a temporary placement with you. You'd have to file paperwork for a permanent placement and the parents would have to surrender the child to the system." Beatrice's face showed she was deep in thought.

"I don't think that will be a problem. The father is in lockup for beating and trying to shoot the kid, and the mother spat on the ground and told me not to bring him back," Hector said dryly.

"They'd still have to sign the paperwork, although I'd recommend taking him out of the home because of the hostility of the household to homosexuals. He is gay, right?" she asked as if she had to make sure Hector was telling her the truth.

"He told me he was. What precipitated this was Matteo's father catching him on the Internet visiting a site with male swimsuit models. He's only ten, but he's already into puberty, which explains the male models. He wanted to see if they had hair down there, too."

Beatrice shook her head. "If the mother and father are rabid homophobes, who was the kid supposed to ask? Of course he went online to look."

Aden joined them. "Fernandez is keeping him overnight to check for a concussion. He's going to be sorer in the morning than he is now. I think it's dawned on him that he no longer has a home. Someone needs to speak to him." Aden eyed Beatrice.

"Beatrice, you go talk to Matteo." Hector took out his cell. "I'll call my roommate and tell him we're about to have company. Aden, could you get me the kid's sizes? I can send Steele to Walmart for some clothing until I can get Matteo's from his mother. The father tried to fire on my deputy. He may not get out on bail." And, with that, Hector acquired a foster son.

Chapter Two

Tuesday, Early Evening

Hector called Steele's cell. "Steele. It's Hector. I'm at the UNM Sandoval Medical Center."

"You all right?" Hector could hear the panic in Steele's voice. Maybe their being together wasn't so impossible after all. He smiled.

"I'm fine. I picked up a late call, child abuse of a gay kid here in Rio Rancho. The father was kicking the kid with steel-toed boots in front of the house and tried to shoot him twice."

Steele whistled. "These lawns are nothing but rocks. He was beating a kid laid out on stones, and then tried to shoot him, the bastard. I hope you're throwing the book at him."

"Yeah, I had Edwards take him to the lockup after they patched him up at UNM. He aimed his gun at Edwards after he tried to shoot the kid twice. I had to shoot the gun out of his hand. The only reason he missed was he was high. He'll be arraigned in the morning. The mother will probably post bail. She told me not to bring the kid back home."

"Shit, from what I understand, it's hard to get someone to take in a gay teen." Steele's voice softened. "What are you going to do?"

"*We're* going to take him in tonight, and I'm going to try to get CYFD to let me provide him with a foster home. If I don't, he'll go to a group home and have the shit beat out of him for the next eight years. If you're not on board, you'll have to find another place to live." Hector warned.

"Of course I'm on board. I was certified as a foster parent in LA. What do you want me to do?" Steele answered. "Poor kid. I've been there, done that, and made the movie. Fortunately, I didn't come out until after college, then I got banned from the Adams homestead." A hint of bitterness tinged Steele Adams' voice.

"Aden's going to call you with clothing sizes. Go to Walmart and get some underwear, shirts, jeans, socks, and a warm coat plus pajamas, a robe, slippers, and a pair of cheap sneakers on your way home tonight. I'll get him better stuff later, or we'll retrieve his own tomorrow or the next day. I'm already qualified as a foster parent. You'll have to get certified here."

"That shouldn't be a problem. I'll retake the classes and send for my paperwork. When did you do that? Qualify as a foster parent, I mean," Steele's voice conveyed his curiosity.

"Before you arrived, I knew about the dearth of foster parents for gay teens and I went through the process. Once you moved in, I didn't actively pursue it, but I'm already qualified." Hector paced.

"I wish you would have asked. I got the certification for the same reason you did, the lack of foster parents for gay kids."

Hector huffed. "You should have seen the kid, Steele, trying to be brave after being shot at and having the shit beat out of him on the lawn."

"Should I make dinner?" Both Hector and Steele had learned how to cook. Having experienced Aden's dinners, they were reluctant to go back to takeout. They got simple recipes from Aden and had graduated to more sophisticated food. Hector even got a few recipes for Mexican food from his mama.

"No, they're keeping him overnight to check him for a concussion. If you could pick up the clothing, I'll bring him home in the morning as soon as he's released from the hospital."

Hector was about to hang up when Steele asked, "You coming home to get some sleep?"

"I'll see how it goes. I may stay with the kid."

"I'll call the office and make sure I'm at the house in the morning." Steele headed up the FBI office in Albuquerque and hadn't taken a day off since he moved to Hector's from his Los Angeles loft.

"So you'll be home?" Hector asked, surprised on how supportive Steele was of Hector bringing a kid into the house on such short notice.

"I'll have the clothes and be ready to cook breakfast. No kid should have to face that alone."

"Good." Hector hesitated. "Thanks for being so positive about all of this."

"You're welcome. I was that kid once," Steele supplied.

"I know. So was I."

Wednesday Morning

At four the next morning, Hector pulled up the

driveway of the Pena home with Deputy Garcia, a poker buddy, right behind him. The father hadn't been released on bail yet, so he knew the mother was alone. He got out of his Explorer and rang the bell with Garcia behind him. The rather blowsy woman from the night before answered the door, dressed but half asleep.

"CYFD has found Matteo a home. I've come for his things." Hector didn't give the woman a chance to object, shamelessly using his uniform to gain access to the boy's room. He and Garcia brought boxes and quickly packed up the boy's clothing and his old laptop computer. There wasn't a toy he could find, only a gaming system held together by duct tape. He slipped it in the bag. Hector would replace it and get him all the other things that boys his age took for granted. Matteo was still a boy even though he was gay, despite what his parents thought.

The sheriff was comfortable. His house was mortgage free, and Steele paid him a minimal rent. He had wisely invested most of his salary for the past fifteen years and now was his chance to give back. After gathering the very few things Matteo' owned, Hector headed for the door. He stopped and nodded to the mother, "Beatrice Marks from CYFD will be here later today to serve you with documents for you to surrender Matteo to the foster system. You might also ask about putting him up for adoption."

"Who'd adopt a ten-year-old fag?" Matteo's mother asked derisively.

"I would," Hector answered quietly. Hector looked around for the brother, but he must have been asleep because he didn't make an appearance.

When Hector returned to the hospital, he had

Matteo's clothes with him. Matteo searched his face with tear-filled eyes.

"I guess they meant it when they said they didn't want me back."

"I want you, Matteo. I'd like you to live with me and my roommate." Hector watched the boy's response carefully.

"Is he gay, too?" Matteo asked gingerly.

"Yes. He works for the FBI." Hector waited for Matteo's reaction.

"A gay FBI agent?" Matteo was incredulous.

"You'd be surprised. Gay men work at all sorts of jobs and live their lives out and proud. Aden, your nurse, does, as does his husband, Dr. Rourke, along with the Special Agent in Charge of the FBI's Albuquerque Division, Steele Adams, and me. You'll meet him later this morning."

Matteo's head shot up as Dr. Fernandez entered the room. "You can get dressed, Matteo. Sheriff Gomez has your clothing. I'm releasing you." Hector glanced at the clock; it was five in the morning. Beatrice Marks, who had been there all night arranging the placement, greeted Hector holding a shaft of papers.

Beatrice Marks followed Hector into the ER cubicle. "I have a judge's order, Matteo, surrendering you to the foster system. I will temporarily place you with Mr. Gomez. If you get along, he'd like the placement to become permanent. Is this okay with you?"

Matteo shrugged. "I'm ten. I don't have much of a choice."

"Steele and I will treat you well, Matteo. There will be rules and school, but other than that, you can play sports, make friends, and be open about your sexuality."

"Do I still have to go to Eagle Ridge. They're all going to know what happened."

"No, we live in the section of town that goes to Mountain View. You'll be able to start fresh. Also, there will be counseling about your options as an LGBT youth. Let's get going to the house. Both Steele and I have the day off, so we can help you get settled."

***

Despite the early hour, Steele was waiting for them at the door. Hector and Matteo got out of the Explorer and made their way to Steele. "Matteo, I'm Steele Adams, Hector's roommate. When Hector called and told me you were coming, I made some pancakes, eggs, and bacon for breakfast. Interested?"

Matteo smiled shyly and nodded his head.

"Come on in and we'll fill up a plate. After you eat, I'll show you your room. It's kind of plain right now, but you can decorate it however you wish. I bought you some temporary clothes from Walmart if you want to go upstairs and change. We'll go to Cottonwood Mall tomorrow. I'm off till after New Year's." Steele smiled widely.

Hector raised his eyebrows. When Steele said he was onboard, Hector had no idea he'd be so enthusiastic. Steele took them to the kitchen where breakfast was waiting with freshly squeezed juice.

Thirty minutes later, Matteo pushed away from the table. "Thank you, I'm full."

Steele turned to Hector. "I put him upstairs. We have another two empty rooms next to that one, so he can have a place to chill. We also have the bonus room on the first floor where we can set up some video games and use it as a playroom.

"Come on, Matteo. I'll show you your room. I put you in the middle. There is a forty-inch flat screen in the room to the right. We have DirecTV, but your viewing times will be limited to no more than an hour and a half a night. You need to pull up your grades to get into college." Steele had the boy follow him upstairs.

"How do you know about my grades?" Matteo asked, suspicion ripe in his voice.

"I'm an FBI agent. We have ways of finding out this kind of thing. You should take a nap; you seem to be tired."

The boy nodded his head.

Hector felt like he'd been run over by a truck. *Why did Steele put the Matteo upstairs when I told him to put the kid in the second downstairs bedroom?*

Steele came down. "Matteo is putting his clothing away. He was glad to see his computer, but he needs a new one and a phone. We need to talk. Let's go out on the patio."

Hector opened a can of Coke and followed him out into the yard.

Steve regarded him gravely. "You've put us in the middle of a drug sting. The senior Pena worked as a distributor for the Mexican cartel and was branching out on his own. You know the cartel has moved their operation to Albuquerque after the Denver fiasco. There is another kid, right?"

"Yeah, Matteo's younger brother, Felipe. How did you know?"

"Sanchez did all the research for the bust. There is no other family. The mother is heavily involved in her husband's business; both are addicts. They're going away for years because, basically, they ran a drug warehouse in their home. CYFD will take the boy. As soon as Manuel gets out on bail this morning, the FBI is arresting him and his wife for possession with intent to distribute. They kept the cocaine and the meth in the garage." He took a swig of Hector's Coke.

"Matteo is going to be upset. As soon as this happens, we'll have to talk to him. Has anyone from your office notified Beatrice Marks?"

"I don't think so. Maybe Rivers from the DEA did. It's a joint task force but mostly their operation." Steele sat on the picnic bench, rolling the Coke can between his hands.

"When is this going down?" Hector glanced down at his watch.

"It's eight-thirty. They were supposed to go in at five."

"Jesus, Edwards and I went to get the kid's clothing at four-thirty. We just missed them. His brother, Felipe, is going to be caught up in all that. Let me call Beatrice. We'll take him. He should be placed with Matteo." Hector picked up his phone.

He put Beatrice on speaker. "I just did an intake on Matteo's brother. I assume that's why you're calling. Do you think his parents will release him?"

"They're going to jail. They don't have much choice, at least for now."

Hector could hear Beatrice tapping her pencil on her desk blotter. "Matteo says they abuse both of them." He wanted to make Matteo happy and get Felipe out of a dangerous situation.

"I'll have to take statements and start an investigation. With both of them in jail, it should be easier to get the neighbors to talk," Beatrice speculated. "I'll call you later today. I have some paperwork to do before you can pick the boy up. You said Steele is certified in LA?"

"Yeah, that's what he said."

"That should make it easier." Beatrice sighed. "This is only an emergency placement until I get Mr. Adams' documentation from California."

"Thanks, Beatrice. I appreciate anything you can do to make this possible." Hector ended the call. "I have to talk to Matteo."

"Don't get his hopes up. It isn't going to be easy to get them to let go of the son who isn't gay." Steele shook his head.

"Depends on what you guys have on them," Hector speculated.

"Enough to put them away for forty years or longer. That is, if they don't cop a plea," Steele said. "But they're going to get out on bail. It wouldn't be good if they could waltz in here in a few days and take Felipe away from his brother."

"I assume Matteo is taking the nap you suggested. I have some things to do besides picking up Felipe. We have to do school transfers—it's good we're in the same school district—and get the foster process started for Felipe. I won't tell Matteo until it's a done deal." Hector gazed at Steele, wondering what more he had to say.

"I'll send for my paperwork from LA and pay to have them overnight it to Beatrice. You have to give me the address. We have something else to discuss. Last night, after you called, I moved my things down into your bedroom." Steele had a catch in his voice.

Hector made a noise but couldn't seem to speak.

"Why are you so surprised? That's where we've been heading for six months now. I'm finally saying aloud what I've been thinking for a while. I want us to be a couple, really together, not just fuck buddies. If we work at it, we could have something like what Aden and Dare have, complete with kids. I know it isn't the most romantic time to say this, but I'm already in love with you. I have been for a while. We could even get a dog." Steele chuckled.

"We've never even kissed." Hector objected.

"I can remedy that right now." Steele pulled him off the picnic bench and into his arms. He nibbled at Hector's lips until they opened to him then Steele deepened the kiss. '

Pushing away, Hector mused, "I must admit we have a certain chemistry."

His cell phone rang. He glanced at the face. "It's Beatrice. I've got to take this." He put it on speaker. "Hello Beatrice, we're on speaker, Steele is with me. Matteo is upstairs getting some sleep."

"Felipe, Matteo's brother is available for fostering. Are you interested?"

"Of course, but you knew that already. I even have a separate bedroom for him."

"I had the CYFD get a judge to give you temporary custody of Felipe because you already had his brother. They were cooking meth somewhere in the house; the agents are still attempting to find where. If they find that lab, I have them on child endangerment. I think Matteo knows more than he's saying." Beatrice sounded disgusted.

"Steele told me about the bust."

"Ms. Marks, this is Steele Adams. Does the DEA want to question Matteo? If they do, I'm going to insist that both Hector and I be present."

"They probably will want to find out what he knows, if anything. I'll let you know and tell them your stipulation. Let me make a note." Hector could hear Beatrice tapping on the computer keyboard.

"We have to tell Matteo what just went down and assure him Felipe is all right, so if there is no other business, Hector will pick up Felipe at noon," Steel told her. "You should have the paperwork done by then, I assume. You'll have my credentials by tomorrow morning."

"We'll have it finished by noon. I'm glad I have a placement for Matteo. The fact that you're willing to take Felipe, too, speaks well of both of you. Go and tell the boy he doesn't have to worry about his brother."

"Will do, Beatrice. Have a productive morning." Hector ended the call.

Steele straightened Hector's uniform. "Further discussion on the other subject can take place this evening. We've got to go upstairs and relieve that poor kid's mind about his brother."

Chapter Three

Wednesday, Late Morning

Hector sat on the side of the bed and gently shook Matteo's shoulder. The boy opened his eyes. "I have some news about Felipe...."

Matteo sat up abruptly. "They didn't hurt him, did they? I should have gotten him out...."

"No, son, he's not hurt. There was a drug bust at your house, and Felipe was brought into CYFD. Beatrice Marks called. You two are going to be placed here together."

"Really, you're not shitting me? Felipe gets to come with me? They hurt us. I tried to protect him, but they hurt me all the time." Matteo sniffled. "He's safe...he's really safe.

"I was going to leave here and run away with him, only I couldn't figure out where to go. Thank you. I know what they were doing. We could have been hurt, bad. I tried to tell my teachers, but no one would listen." Matteo cried.

Steele stood at the door to the bedroom. "Someone listened. The DEA and FBI were over there this morning. Your parents are going to prison. You're going to have to deal with that."

"I'd rather deal with that than have my baby brother find and take some of their fucking drugs."

"You're going to have to learn to watch your mouth. My son doesn't speak that way to his elders." Hector's face turned stern.

"Don't throw us out. I promise I'll clean up my act." Matteo panicked.

"I wouldn't throw you out, but you might find yourself doing extra chores," Hector said in a matter-of-fact voice.

"Can we go get Felipe now?"

"I have to go by myself. You're going with Steele to the mall, Best Buy, Costco, and Walmart to get a few necessities because you're back in school after Thanksgiving." Hector glanced up at Steele. He nodded. "Also, while you're waiting for me, make a Christmas list for you and your brother. You won't have anything more from your old house, so think on what needs to be replaced. On second thought, you should make it together. There are some things you might like to share."

Steele, still leaning on the doorframe, spoke. "That list should be a pie-in-the-sky list, anything you ever wanted."

Matteo's eyes lit up. "Will we have Thanksgiving dinner and a Christmas tree and everything? My parents were too busy with their business to ever do anything like that."

Hector's eyes shot to Steele's. A brief flash of anger, quickly covered, broke out across his partner's face. Hector was startled at his thought. Steele was, in fact, his partner now. Tonight, they'd talk after they got the boys to bed. Dozens of things needed to be hammered out: the status of their relationship, finances, care of the boys. He was dizzy with the implications of Steele moving into his bedroom.

Hector pulled into the parking lot of CYFD, noting Beatrice Mark's red Ford Focus in her assigned space. Still in uniform, he strode into the building and told the admin he had an appointment with Beatrice at noon. He found Felipe sitting on a metal chair with a hastily packed bag of clothes and a beat-up teddy bear with a ripped ear. The boy's eyes were red and swollen. Hector stopped to speak with him.

He knelt, and the boy gazed at him with tear-filled eyes. "You took Matteo yesterday. Can I go where he is? I missed him. Mama beat me because I cried all night."

"I have to go in and see Ms. Marks, but I think that can be arranged," Hector reassured the small boy. Peeking out from under the long sleeve of his shirt, Hector saw bruises.

"Roll up your sleeve, son," Hector asked gently.

Felipe panicked. "I was bad. I didn't shut up like she said. If you take me to Matteo, I'll be quiet as a mouse."

Hector's mouth set in a grim line. Grabbing Felipe by the hand, he knocked on the door to Beatrice's office. He walked inside. Without preamble, he rolled up the sleeve of Felipe's thin shirt. "Did you see this?"

Beatrice picked up her head. "No, I didn't, and it puts a different complexion on this business. I was worried that I'd have to return him after they got out on bail. This makes it so I don't have to. I can file charges on his behalf." Beatrice stood and went looking for her camera. "I'm going to take photos and then you can take him home."

"Home to Matteo?" The boy's eyes lit up in excitement.

"Yes, home to Matteo and my partner, Steele." Felipe smiled.

***

Matteo surprised Steele. They left the house at ten and went to several stores. When Steele would ask him what he wanted, the kid said, "Felipe needs this," or "Felipe would love that."

The kid didn't have a selfish bone in his body. Steele purchased what Felipe needed but also made sure Matteo got his fair share. Steele was rather surprised. He knew that he liked the idea of being a dad because he'd filled out the paperwork and taken the classes in LA before he came to Albuquerque. The fact that Hector had also applied to be a foster parent was interesting. He liked the idea of sharing the position of dad with Hector.

"Let's go.... Hector should be home soon. We'll do the rest of the shopping tomorrow and Friday. What would you like for dinner?"

"What can I have?" Matteo was obviously taken aback by the question.

"I can grill hamburgers, steak, or chicken. I can make meatballs and spaghetti. You can help make meatballs, if you like. We'll have salad, and I'll buy some ice cream for dessert." Steele watched Matteo's eyes.

"Meatballs. Felipe likes meatballs and spaghetti. You're talking about real meatballs, not the kind that come with spaghetti in a can."

"Real meatballs...I promise." Steele chuckled.

"I can help?" Matteo's eyes lit up.

"Of course you can help. Boys need to know how to cook, too. When you get older, how will you feed yourself if you don't know how to cook? It gets very expensive to buy takeout all of the time, believe me, I know. And you won't get the kind of food you need to be strong." Steele held the boy's steady regard.

"You'll teach me so I can show Felipe?" Matteo asked.

"How about we both teach Felipe?" Steele ruffled the boy's hair as they got out of the car at Albertsons.

It took them thirty minutes at Albertsons to pick up the ingredients for dinner and a few staples. They were home by one. Steele and Matteo had just finished putting away all of their purchases when Hector arrived with Felipe.

"Matteo...." Felipe burst into tears.

"Are you okay?" Matteo started an inspection of his brother. Felipe wrapped his arms around his waist and wouldn't let Matteo see.

"Felipe...." Matteo warned.

Felipe unclenched his arms, and Matteo drew up his shirtsleeves. "Bitch," Matteo said succinctly as he examined the black-and-blue marks left from his mother's pinches and slaps.

"I'm sorry, Matteo. I know you told me to go into the house and be quiet, but I couldn't stop crying. I was worried about you. I thought they'd put you somewhere I would never find you again." Felipe started to sniffle.

Matteo hugged his brother, hard. "We'll both be okay now. We're going to stay with Hector and Steele. I went out today with Steele and we bought you clothes and stuff, and he's going to teach us how to make meatballs and spaghetti. It's going to be good, I promise."

"Can you show me the clothes and stuff and tell me where I'm going to sleep? I don't need my own bed. I can sleep with Matteo." Felipe nervously looked around to watch the adult's faces.

"Your bedroom is right next to mine. We share a bathroom. It's neat." Matteo moved his eyes to meet Steele's. "Do I have time to show my brother his stuff before we make the meatballs?"

"Yes, you do. But come down right afterward or we'll be eating very late."

"Okay." Matteo went to race up the stairs after Felipe but quickly turned around, ran up first to Hector then to Steele and gave them each a quick kiss on the cheek. He whispered, "Thank you," then followed Felipe up the stairs.

"That is one good kid. We went shopping, and all he was interested in was making sure his brother had what he needed. He was more excited about the things his brother got than he was about his own." Steele sat at the kitchen table.

"They've never had Christmas or Thanksgiving." Hector frowned.

"Nothing. Matteo said his parents were too busy with their *business*. And Felipe thought Santa didn't know where they lived. Matteo convinced him it wasn't because he was a bad boy that Santa didn't come," Steele said dryly.

Steele stood. "I've got to call Aden and Dare later and ask if there is room at the table for two more for Thanksgiving. Knowing Aden, it won't be a problem." Hector read over Beatrice's paperwork while Steele assembled the things they would need to make meatballs and marinara sauce.

"We have to buy more Christmas decorations. I only have a few for a small tree. We have fourteen-foot ceilings; that's one big-ass tree if we want to fill up the space. I hope you have a long ladder in storage," Hector thought out loud.

"I have a ladder and some Christmas stuff in Smart Storage, and we can split the cost of the new decorations. We have to talk about money after the boys go to bed." Steele chopped a couple of onions, some garlic, and soaked white bread in a milk and egg mixture. He went into the spice cabinet and found a jar labeled Italian Seasoning and added that to the bowl along with the meat.

Hector felt his eyes go wide. *Steele really means it. He wants to try to make a go of our relationship as something more than fuck buddies.* Aloud, he said, "We'll need to shop this weekend, before Black Friday, or else there'll be nothing left. I want to order an enormous piñata online. This year, those kids are going to have a Christmas."

Hector automatically opened a couple of cans of Italian plum tomatoes, tomato puree, and paste and started chopping onions, garlic, parsley, a bay leaf, and fresh basil for the sauce.

Gingerly, Matteo stuck his head into the kitchen. "Uh...could I help now, Steele? Felipe fell asleep. I covered him up. He didn't sleep much last night."

"Felipe should sleep. We'll make the meatballs, and next time you can help me show him. Hector's making the sauce. Watch what ingredients he uses from the counter and how he puts them in the pot."

Matteo carefully examined the cans and the spice jars. "How much of each?" He cocked his head at Hector.

"Here I'll show you."

Matteo spent the next ten minutes studying the amount of spices that Steele put in the meatballs and that Hector put in the sauce.

Matteo sat on the kitchen stool by Steele. "Mix the ingredients together with clean hands then take out an ice cream scoop to make them uniform in size. Take each meatball and roll it around in the palm of your hands like this, until it's round." Steel demonstrated the technique.

"What do we do next?" Matteo asked.

"Next, we pour some olive oil in the skillet and brown the meatballs on all sides. That way, they won't fall apart in Hector's sauce." Steele heated the oil until it sizzled, then he turned down the gas jet under the skillet and began to place the meatballs.

A few minutes later he took a slotted spoon and turned the meatballs to brown evenly. "Here, you try...."

Matteo furrowed his brow, took the spoon, put a meatball in the oil, and turned a few others.

"That's it. Now you know how to make meatballs," Steele teased.

"Tell me again how much bread and milk and egg you use?"

Hector smiled, Steele and Matteo were doing fine. "I'm going upstairs to check on Felipe."

"Thank you. I was just going to do that." Matteo's face fell as he realized he'd forgotten about his brother. Hector scowled and shook his head. He knew who'd been the surrogate parent in the Pena household.

The sheriff walked up the stairs and opened the door of the fourth bedroom. Felipe had fallen asleep with two bears, one old Winnie the Pooh with a torn ear and a missing eye, the second a brand new Pooh bear from J.C. Penny, if the bag on the floor was anything to go by.

He was dressed in some new pajamas, the robe and the slippers placed neatly at the end of the bed. *How could anyone be hateful to these kids?* Hector felt a little dampness near the corner of his eye and quickly wiped it away.

He came down the stairs as Steele explained how they had to put the meatballs in the sauce to continue cooking and soak in the flavor. He watched, smiling as Matteo carefully took the meatballs out of the skillet, drained them on a paper towel, and then transferred them to the pot full of marinara sauce.

Steele drew in his gaze. "We'll make the spaghetti when Felipe wakes up," he told Matteo. What his eyes told Hector were, "I'll speak to you later."

***

Hector went into the bedroom to change out of his uniform and lock away his weapon. He had told White, Edwards, and Garcia he was taking the rest of the week off as long as they had coverage. He noticed that Steele's Glock was already in the gun case. The empty closet was filled with Steele's dress shirts and suits. The high chest of drawers from Steele's bedroom now resided next to his. He must have gotten John from across the street to help him move it down.

Hector went into the bathroom and found Steele's electric razor charging on the vanity and his toiletries in the second medicine cabinet. Steele had made himself at home. Considering how he thought things were going just yesterday, he considered his mood and found he was happy. Before Steele, he'd been content, but now, with Steele and the two boys, he was happy. He chuckled at himself for being such a sap and changed into a pair of jeans and a sweatshirt reading UNM. He came out into the kitchen.

"Matteo, why don't you take a nap, too. You didn't sleep much in the hospital last night." Hector started to make a pot of coffee.

"I can still help. Do you need any chores done?" Matteo asked.

Steele sat him down at the kitchen table. "Son, you don't have to sing for your supper. We want you to be happy here. If you're not tired, go to the great room and watch TV, but nothing that isn't PG-13 unless Hector or I approve." Matteo nodded.

"If you don't need me to do anything, maybe I will take a nap. I am kind of sleepy. Is that okay? I'll leave Felipe's and my doors open in case he cries out because he's waking up in a strange place. Thank you for everything, especially for getting Felipe out of there. I was scared." He got up from the chair, pushed it back under the table, and wearily climbed the stairs."

Chapter Four

Wednesday, Late Afternoon

Hector poured both himself and Steele a cup of coffee. He pulled his chin up and examined Steele's eyes. "You realize that you committed to those boys and to me today."

"I've wanted to commit to you for a while now. I thought you weren't interested, that maybe you were still carrying a torch for Aden."

Hector chuckled. "Dare would have my balls for breakfast." He met Steele's stare. "You're serious. After all these months, you thought I still carried a torch for Aden. I haven't seen Aden that way since before you moved into this house. I've wanted you. I was waiting for some sign that you wanted me, too, for something besides bedroom games." Hector shrugged.

"When Matteo showed up, I saw my chance and took it. If you told me I couldn't move into the bedroom with you, I would have moved out. I couldn't be here anymore, not knowing where I stood." Steele poured some half and half into his coffee.

"I was thinking the same thing yesterday morning. I have a feeling that the physical side of things is about to get a lot more intimate. I'm a cuddler," he deadpanned.

Steele laughed out loud. "Sometimes the best part of sex is the cuddling afterward. He stood and kissed Hector. I'm going into the office and getting a pad. We need to make a Christmas list."

"Do you think we could manage to make Christmas dinner? The boys should stay home for our first Christmas together. We can invite Dare, Aden, and Debra. That way, if we start to screw up the meal, salvation is at hand." Hector took a sip of his coffee. "This is decent coffee. Our brewing skills have improved."

"We should invite Sanchez for the holidays. He has no family. I was going to ask Dare and Aden if we could bring him for Thanksgiving." Steele went to find his cell phone.

"Give them a call. I promised Aden an update on Matteo anyway. He was concerned that the kid would have to go back to those pieces of pond scum they called parents." Hector yawned.

"All I have to do is cut the vegetables for the salad, baby. I'm going to make a box of brownies, and they can have them with the ice cream and fudge sauce I bought with Matteo at Albertsons. You were probably up most of the night, too. Go take a nap. I'll call Aden and I'll wake you and the boys up for dinner." Steele gave him a quick kiss.

Hector walked into the bedroom and lay on top of the bed. *Baby, huh? I could get used to this new paradigm.*

***

"Dare, it's Steele."

"What can I do for you?" Dare seemed amicable.

"I know Aden told you about Matteo. We ran drug busts today in Albuquerque and Rio Rancho. Matteo's parents were distributors. This morning, Hector picked up Matteo's brother who we are also going to foster and maybe try to adopt along with Matteo. What I'm calling about is that these kids have never had a Thanksgiving or Christmas."

"What?" Dare sounded incredulous.

"Yeah, Matteo had to convince Felipe, the five-year-old, that he wasn't a bad boy, that Santa lost their address. Anyway, we want to do it up grand for the boys this year. Can we bring the boys and Sanchez to you for Thanksgiving and have Christmas here? Of course, we'll also invite Debra and Sanchez for Christmas. Sanchez has no family." Steele knew the soft heart he hid was there in his voice, but he didn't care. These kids were going to have fabulous holidays, complete with Debra as their unofficial grandmother.

"Children always make the holidays special. I'm not going back to Atlanta because my family was out here for the wedding not too long ago. The kids and Sanchez are welcome for Thanksgiving. But, since Aden is doing the cooking, let me check."

"Dork," Steele heard Aden say in the background. "Of course the kids and Jerry Sanchez are welcome. You know I'll cook, and Mom will bring another whole meal. Ask them what we can bring for Christmas."

"You heard him. Just let us know what to bring. Make a list of what you want to serve and we'll divide it up. That way your first company meal won't be that difficult," Dare suggested.

"Why don't you guys bring the pies. Hector and I still haven't gotten the knack of getting the crust flaky rather than hard. We can do the rest of it and have the boys help. It will be a bonding experience. Today, Matteo and I made meatballs."

"Sounds like you're falling in love with those boys." Dare chuckled.

"You know, I took the oldest out shopping and most of the stuff he wanted was for his brother. He didn't pick out much for himself," Steele told Dare, still amazed by the boy not taking advantage.

"Obviously not a greedy kid," Dare commented.

"The only thing he insisted on getting was a new teddy bear for his brother. He bought him a used Winnie the Pooh from a thrift shop two years ago. He was afraid the officers wouldn't let Felipe bring the bear once we told him about the bust. Matteo bought that kid the only present he ever got from change he saved up from taking out the trash for a neighbor. Felipe is upstairs sleeping with a bear in each arm. The DEA Agent, Jonathan Rivers, let the kid take the bear instead of putting it into evidence." Steele was still trying to control his anger over the trauma the boys had lived through.

"Sounds like a decent human being." Dare shouted to Aden, "Put a set of toy trains on the Christmas list. Those boys are going to enjoy this Christmas."

"My sentiments, exactly. I have to make the salad and garlic bread, and I promised Matteo I'd wake him to help with the spaghetti."

"Steele, before you go, don't let Matteo near the boiling water except to put the spaghetti in the pot. My brother's kid burned himself. It was so bad it blistered. Drain it yourself," the doctor in Dare spoke up.

"Thanks, I didn't think of that. I don't want him in the emergency room the first night we have him. Bad enough they both arrived black and blue from abuse. Beatrice Marks documented all of Felipe's injuries and Aden, Matteo's, while he was in the ER. I'd run with the kids before I'd give them back to their parents," Steele said adamantly.

"They must have been in bad shape for you to consider breaking the law." Dare whistled.

"The little guy's arms were black and blue from slaps and pinches because he cried when the parents threw the brother out. His back and legs were marked by a belt. But they were practiced abusers. Nothing showed. It was all under the clothing. On top of that, Matteo always worried they'd leave drugs around that Felipe would think were candy." Steele's voice was hard.

"What scum! Don't worry, we'll all make sure they have a great holiday season this year," Aden shouted in the background.

"Sorry about that. You're on speaker," Dare said wryly.

"I haven't discussed it with Hector yet, but I want to get them a dog; not as big a dog as Ranger and Monk, but maybe a Beagle or a Shetland sheepdog. I have to do some research to find out what are the best breeds for kids." Steele bounced the idea off Dare and Aden.

"Hector always plays with Ranger and Monk when he's here. I don't think he'll object. What about you guys? Any progress on the relationship front?" Dare asked, snickering.

Steele's voice grew husky. "As a matter of fact,

yes. I moved into the master bedroom last night. We discussed it, and we're ready to take our relationship to the next level. Frankly, I'm in love with him but just worked up the courage to tell him today."

"Don't tell us. Let him know how you feel, repeatedly, until he believes it. My God, both of you are such dorks. I'm making Dare hang up. I'm getting dinner on the table and you have spaghetti to make. We'll talk tomorrow. Say good night, Dare."

"Yes, dear. I've got to go. My lover wants me, and I'm going to have him over the kitchen table," Dare said in a sinister voice.

"That's a visual I didn't need with my dinner." Steele laughed. "Good night guys." He ended the call.

***

Steele went back into the kitchen and cut up the vegetables for a salad. Putting it in the refrigerator, Steele turned on the oven and whipped up the box of brownies. Hector came out of the bedroom rubbing his eyes. "Dinner will be ready in thirty minutes. I've got to get the boys up. Matteo wanted to help me make the spaghetti."

"I'll go up and get them. The meatballs and the sauce smell good. We work well together," Hector observed.

"Yes, we do." Steele gave him a tiny peck on the lips and went back to his preparations.

Matteo came bounding down the stairs with a smile on his face. "Felipe is getting washed up for dinner. Thank you. He really liked the stuff we bought him. I'm glad they let him bring his bear. Do you think we could wash it for him and fix his ear and eye? Can I help with the spaghetti?"

"I think we can manage to sew on an ear, and we can look for new eyes at Michaels. I have to go there for ribbon for the tree anyway. "So, yes to all three requests. I put the water on to boil with some salt and a tiny bit of olive oil. We'll put the spaghetti in the boiling water and keep checking it to see if it's done. Put the spaghetti in, spreading it around the rim of the pot. As it softens, you stir it down into the water."

After about eight minutes passed, Steele took a strand of spaghetti out and gave half to Matteo to taste and kept half for himself. "Taste. It should be soft with a little bite."

Matteo tasted and nodded his head.

"This is done. Now you have to move out of the way so you don't get burned while I drain the noodles." Steele pulled out the colander and drained the pot, putting the spaghetti back in the pot with a little of Hector's sauce and twirling it around.

Hector took out a platter and, using a pair of tongs, spread the pasta over the serving dish and spooned sauce and meatballs over the pasta.

Steele served up the salad with Italian dressing and brought out the garlic bread. Felipe came down the stairs. "We're all going to eat together?"

"Of course," Hector returned.

"See, I told you things would be better here," Steele heard Matteo whisper to Felipe.

***

"Matteo, do you remember the nurse from last night?" Hector asked conversationally.

"Aden, his husband was a doctor...." Matteo stared at Hector.

"The reason I brought Aden and Dare up was to

tell you that we're going to have Thanksgiving dinner at their house with Aden's mother and a man from Steele's office, Jerry Sanchez."

Matteo's eyes opened wide. "Will we get turkey and stuffing? Mama usually bought a Swanson turkey dinner, but you're talking about a whole turkey, like on TV, aren't you?"

"Yes, he is, with all the trimmings." Steele added.

Hector continued, "And, Felipe, while you were sleeping, Steele filed an official change of address form with Santa through the FBI, so there will be no more mistakes on where you're living on Christmas."

"For Matteo, too?"

Hector chuckled, "For Matteo, too. Now I want both of you to make up lists of what you want from Santa. It seems he's got to make up for a lot of missed Christmases. Tomorrow, we're going shopping for Christmas lights for outside the house and decorations for inside and out."

"Will we get *luminarias*?" Matteo asked. Then put his hand over his mouth as if he'd asked too much.

"I think that can be arranged, but we have to get the ones with the electric candles because it's been so dry that a spark from a lit candle could spread wildfires."

Matteo nodded his head, transfixed by every word. "Who's working Christmas for you, Hector?" Matteo watched Steele smile gently at the man across the table.

"Hearing the circumstances, White and Garcia volunteered to be on call. I'll have to work the morning shift on Christmas Eve, seven to three; however, after that, I'm off until eleven on the twenty-sixth. But on Thanksgiving, I'm on call."

"I called in a few favors. I'm off until New Year's unless we have a crisis," Steele told Hector. "Then we'll split tree and outside light duty. I suppose we're going to outdo all of the neighbors?"

"Of course...." Matteo saw a spark of something in Hector's eye.

"I wouldn't have it any other way, baby." Matteo was startled at the endearment.

"You two are together like Aden and his doctor husband?" he asked.

"We're live together, but we're not married." Hector answered.

"Yet," said Steele. Matteo watched as Steele gave Hector a wide smile.

"Yet," Hector agreed. He smiled back at Steele.

Matteo was a smart boy. For him and his brother to survive in the atmosphere they came from, he had to be. He heard an undercurrent to the conversation; a vein of veiled seduction lying under the conversation between the two men, very satisfied with themselves and each other.

"Can we help clean up?" Matteo asked.

"Not tonight. You two need some rest." Hector yawned.

"Felipe, neither one of us got enough sleep last night. Why don't we shower, you can change back into your pajamas, and maybe we could work on those lists for Santa, if Steele and Hector have some paper and a pen."

Felipe gave Steele and Hector a shy kiss. "Thank you for giving me back my brother," Felipe told them quietly.

Matteo nodded. "Thank you for everything. We'll be asleep by nine."

The boys went up the stairs to their rooms.

***

Hector started to clean the table and stack dishes in the dishwasher. Steele came up behind him and kissed his neck. Hector turned into his arms. "We need to talk."

"Agreed. I'll make some coffee and finish the clean-up. The boys weren't the only ones who didn't sleep well last night." Steele finished loading the dishwasher and set the timer to start it at one in the morning. He ground some beans, brought out some bottled water to put in the reservoir, and put on the coffee.

Hector got out two mugs and the sugar along with the carton of half and half. The two men sat across from each other at the kitchen table.

Chapter Five

Wednesday Evening

H ector leaned back in his chair. "What was it about Matteo's arrival that had you moving into my bedroom?"

"I've always wanted to be in your bedroom, even when we were in Dare's guesthouse. But while we were in the guesthouse, all you could see was Aden; even though it was evident that Aden only had eyes for Dare. I was giving you time to get used to the idea of you and me together. The boy's arrival accelerated my plans and gave me an opening."

Hector raised a skeptical eyebrow. "We've been fucking for months. Why didn't you say something then?" He prepared his coffee.

"Because you couldn't decide if you wanted me that way. I left your bed every time we had sex, waiting for you to invite me to stay. This is your house, Hector. You needed to tell me not to bother hunting for an apartment. You had to be the one who made the first move. But you didn't." Steele's eyes got a little glassy.

"What precipitated you moving into my bed?"

Hector prepared his coffee.

"The boys did. Matteo did. He needs stability. I decided to force your hand. Was I wrong to think you may want more from me than a good fuck?" Steele's blue eyes were arresting in their intensity.

Hector sighed. "No, you weren't wrong. Just yesterday morning, I decided to ask if you wanted a relationship, and, if you didn't, I planned to ask you to leave. I couldn't handle the uncertainty."

"We've been two fools. Each of us held off, thinking that the other would make the first move. I decided to stop being foolish and act. Are you angry?" Steele's eyes pleaded with Hector for understanding.

"How can I be angry when it's what I wanted, too? We have feelings we need to explore. Now that we have the boys, we need to be sure of where we stand with each other so they know where they stand with us." Hector glanced up the stairs.

"I've never spoken about my finances with you. I sold my LA loft for cash. I've been saving about seventy percent of my salary for years and have an impressive portfolio and a good income from some rental properties I own in Chicago and LA. I can afford to more than help provide for the boys. They need so much. I can set up a college fund, and we can add to it." Hector got up and examined the small amount of laundry in the basket in the laundry room off the kitchen.

"I own a share in several local businesses and have a healthy portfolio. Would it be presumptuous of me to suggest mingling our funds?" Hector felt like he was walking on eggs.

"No, I'm in this for the long haul. Eventually, I'd like us to marry when we're surer of what we have together." Hector frowned at the holes in Felipe's long-sleeved shirt.

Steele's eyes followed him. "I know, Felipe's clothing. Matteo came with nothing worth saving; Felipe came with next to nothing." Steele took the shirt from Hector. All of his underwear is so thin you can see through it. His T-shirts are much the same. His winter coat is too light, and he doesn't own a hat and gloves."

"They don't have toys, not even a bicycle. Matteo had an old gaming system, but you could tell that it was bought used. It's held together with duct tape. He must have bought it the same way he bought Felipe the bear—at a thrift shop. He did chores for neighbors to get the money," Hector said in disgust. "Let's talk about our relationship in bed tonight. The boys need our attention now."

Steele nodded. "Matteo bought that bear for his brother when he was only eight years old himself. I wonder what kind of work he had to do to get that old Atari 400. All of the games he selected were the kind that Felipe could play. He certainly is devoted to his brother."

"His brother was all he had, his only friend. I don't imagine with the drug operation running out of the house that the parents encouraged them to have friends. Why did they have kids they didn't want and refused to take care of? It wasn't as if they didn't have the money." Hector cut into the brownies.

"We should call the boys for dessert. You and the boys were the reason I was saving. I always knew I wanted a husband and kids. You're the one I want, baby. Believe me." Steele was in earnest.

Hector mouthed, "Not now," and moved to the bottom of the stairs. "Who wants brownie sundaes before they go to bed?"

Matteo came down with Felipe. "Really, brownies *and* ice cream? Can we have some? We could share if there isn't enough."

Hector glanced at Steele who had the same grim expression he wore. Matteo must have caught his lips pursing because his face fell. "We don't need ice cream or brownies. We had a good supper."

"The expression on my face had nothing to do with you. It was about a case I'm working."

Matteo's face was all smiles again as Steele put out the brownies and ice cream, heating the fudge sauce in the microwave.

Hector brought out a jar of candied walnuts and a plastic container of chocolate sprinkles, "Who wants walnuts or sprinkles?"

Felipe lifted his eyes to Hector. "Can we have both?"

Matteo spoke sharply. "Don't be greedy...."

"He's not greedy, Matteo. He's a kid. Forget about what you were allowed to have when you lived with your parents. It's different here. We can afford for you to have sprinkles, walnuts, and what's a sundae without whipped cream?"

Steele smiled in evident satisfaction when Matteo's jaw dropped. "Those sundaes won't make themselves. I'll cut the brownies. Matteo, get the ice cream from the freezer and the whipped cream from the fridge. Hector will take out the walnuts and four bowls from the cabinet next to the refrigerator. Felipe can pick up the spoons from the drawer by the oven."

The boys scurried to do his bidding. Steele cut the brownies and slid one into each bowl. Hector scooped out the ice cream and parceled out the walnuts. Then he added the whipped cream and finally the sprinkles. He found a jar of maraschino cherries and put one on top of each sundae.

Steele poured out two glasses of milk and more coffee for Hector and himself. The boys sat down with their bowls, happy and laughing. They hadn't had enough of that in their life. "After you eat, brush your teeth and then it's time for bed."

"Yes, Hector, Steele, thank you for the ice cream and brownies. It was wonderful. It's time for bed, Felipe. You can give us our list of chores tomorrow. Here is our Santa list."

Hector took the list and sat back down at the kitchen table to finish his second mug of coffee. He unfolded the piece of paper. "Read this, *mi corazón*."

Steele's head popped up at the endearment.

"It's just as I suspected. Everything on here is for Felipe. Matteo feels that he isn't worth anything. I need to talk to Beatrice about a child psychologist."

Steele took the list from his hands and ran his eyes over Matteo's careful script. "Yeah, talk to Beatrice."

***

"Matteo, do you think they'll let us stay here? I like it here."

"So do I. Let's be really good so we don't screw up and they make us leave. It seems like they really want us, both of us."

"You don't think Mama and Papi can come back and mess this up for us?" Felipe asked.

"I'm going to tell them all about the drugs and guns tomorrow morning. That way, they'll be in jail so long, they can't take us away from here. Go to your room and get some sleep. I'll make sure nothing bad happens. Haven't I always taken care of you?"

"Yes, you have. But who takes care of you, Matteo? Who takes care of you?" Felipe hugged his brother, kissed him good night, and went to his own room.

***

Steele finished stacking the coffee mugs and the bowls they used for the sundaes in the dishwasher. "You didn't get any sleep last night either. Come on, I'm taking you to bed."

"I like the idea of you taking me to bed and staying through the night. As a matter of fact, I like the idea of you in my bed permanently." Hector leered as Steele grabbed his hand.

Steele spoke so quietly that he had to strain to hear him. "Thank God. I've been waiting so long for you to see me, not the badge or the job, or a buddy—me."

"I see you, Steele. I always have. I didn't think you were interested in anything but scratching an itch by coming to my bed a few times a week. I thought you didn't see me. We have to work on our communication skills, especially now that we have the boys." Hector slid under the covers. Steele followed.

"I'm not going to make love to you tonight because you're tired. When I truly make you mine, I want your full attention, baby.

"You're right, I am tired tonight and I want to focus on you when we finally make love instead of fuck." Hector chuckled.

Steele smacked him on the ass. "I am so going to enjoy tapping that ass with us finally in sync."

"Tomorrow night. It's a date. Now, let's get to

49

sleep. The boys are going to be antsy in the morning."

Thursday Morning

Matteo got up, brushed his teeth, and got dressed. He checked on Felipe who was still sleeping. That was good. With their parents, Felipe never got enough sleep with all the people coming in and out of the house at all hours of the day and night. He always had black circles under his eyes.

Matteo heard Steele and Hector in the kitchen. He deliberately made noise so they would hear him coming in case they were kissing or something.

"Good morning, son. How did you sleep?" Hector asked. "I made scrambled eggs, sausage, and English muffins for breakfast.

"I slept really well. The bed was soft and warm, and I had two sheets and a comforter."

Hector's mouth got tight again; his lips pursed. Matteo quickly backpedaled. "I don't need the sheets if someone else needs them."

"Why did you say that?" Hector asked.

"No reason." He turned away from Hector's eyes and shuffled his feet.

"Don't lie to me, Matteo," Hector said sternly.

"Uh...."

"Go ahead, son. You won't get in trouble." Steele took a sip of his coffee.

"Hector's expression changed. and his lips pursed. At home, it meant I was asking for too much," Matteo explained.

"I frowned because I'm disgusted by the fact that you weren't warm or comfortable at night at your parents' house. It makes me angry."

"I gave my covers to Felipe. We slept in the same room. He was always so cold, and I wasn't allowed to sleep with him to keep him warm. I hope you don't mind, but I didn't wake him. He has nightmares and last night he slept so good. He didn't cry out. I need to talk to you anyway, and he shouldn't have to hear this."

Steele regarded Matteo, concerned. Matteo fidgeted, but his eyes were steady. He sat at the kitchen table with his eyes down, fidgeting. He raised his head to Hector and Steele. "I don't know where to start.

Steele put his arm around the boy's shoulders. "The beginning is a good place."

Steele smiled. Matteo regarded him carefully and started to talk.

"My father and mother aren't good people. They were always trying to hit Felipe, and I couldn't always protect him. That's why I was so worried the other night."

"Did you see them mark him?" Hector hissed through his teeth.

"We were both always black and blue under our clothes. I put him underneath me so he wouldn't get it so bad. He's so little. They've been hitting him since he was two. I tried to shield him, I really did, but sometimes I didn't get there in time or they pulled me off of him."

Steele gave him a hug. "Felipe knows you tried to save him from your parents. He loves you very much."

Matteo's face turned grim. "That wasn't all I had to worry about. There were always drugs and guns in the house, and the guns were left lying all over the place. We even had guns in the bathroom. I had to make sure Felipe didn't think they were toys. I saw on TV what happens to little boys who play with guns and the bas...uh, creep always left them loaded with the safety off."

Steele's face tightened. "It was a good thing that you were there to stop Felipe from playing with them. There could have been a terrible accident." Steele saw Hector's knuckles go white gripping the kitchen table.

Matteo turned to Hector. "I know both of you have guns, but I saw Steele lock up his gun, and I think you do the same. So, even though there are guns in the house, I don't have to worry about them."

"No, son, you don't. I'll show you the gun safe. Unless there is danger, we lock them up every night." Steele reassured him grabbing Hector's hand and mouthing over Matteo's bent head, "Take it easy. It's them, not the kids. He's going to see your face and think you're mad at him."

Matteo continued. "My father used to threaten to shoot us if we didn't do what he asked. We had guns waved in our face at least once a week if not more. She was no better."

Steele watched Hector's lips purse and felt his own tighten.

"I'm not lazy. I didn't mind doing the cooking, cleaning, and taking care of Felipe. At least that way I could make sure he ate and had clean clothes, but I refused to run drugs for my father at school. He beat me regularly for that, but, no matter what he did, I wouldn't take that stuff to school. I told my teachers. I don't know if it was one of them who called your office." Tears began coursing down his cheeks.

Steele opened his arms and Matteo ran into them.

"I didn't want to be a rat. If he knew, he'd kill me for sure, but Felipe thought that clear stuff was candy and the white stuff was sugar. That's what they told him. I was afraid he'd try to steal some of it because we never got sweets unless someone brought them to school."

Steele shuddered, thinking of Felipe lying in the hospital with brain damage or fighting for his life after a drug overdose. Lost in the horrors of his own imagination, he had to forcibly bring himself back to listen to the rest of what Matteo had to say.

"I wanted to tell you. I'll testify in court so that they never get near my brother again. They don't want me."

Steele reached for his phone and handed it to Hector. "Call Beatrice," he said succinctly.

Hector immediately tapped Beatrice's number into the phone. Hector left the kitchen and went into the bedroom. Steele reassured Matteo he'd done the right thing by telling them. He told him to finish his breakfast and then stepped into the great room to call Sanchez and the DEA

Chapter Six

Thursday, Mid-Morning

Jonathan Rivers, the agent in charge of the Albuquerque Office of the Drug Enforcement Administration pulled into Hector's driveway right after Steele opened the door for Sanchez.

Rivers was abrupt. "What have you got for me Adams?"

"The Rio Rancho bust you made yesterday? I have a corroborating witness."

Matteo sat quietly on the couch. Hector had taken Felipe out to shop for Christmas decorations.

"Who?" Rivers snapped.

"Me...." Matteo stood up. "My name is Matteo Pena. You arrested my papi and mama yesterday for drugs. I can tell you where they hid all the guns and the drugs. I know you didn't find all of it. I made sure I knew where it all was so that my little brother couldn't accidently get into the drugs or play with the guns. They told him the heroin was sugar and the meth was candy. I had to keep him safe." He wrung his hands.

"Go ahead, son," Steele encouraged, sitting Matteo down on the couch and seating himself next to the boy. He put his arm around the boy's shoulders.

"He wanted me to sell the stuff at school. I told him no and he beat me up. I kept telling him no. He broke my arm and gave me black eyes, but I wouldn't do it. When the officer came to school and said we should tell a teacher if we saw anyone trying to sell us drugs, I told anyone who would listen about my father." Matteo sniffed. "That was over six months ago."

Steele gave Rivers a lethal glare as if to say *what took you so long?* The doorbell rang and Beatrice Marks arrived.

River's voice softened. "You did the right thing, Matteo. I had to go through the court and build a case; the investigation took a while. Your father had other people who ran drugs, and people he reported to. We had to get all of them."

"I understand. It's okay. Felipe is safe here now." Matteo sniffled. "Check under the wooden floors. They raised them up to be able to hide stuff. All of the walls behind the furniture has stuff beneath the sheet rock, between the studs. If you push on a piece of the molding, it opens up, and you'll see the drugs piled up. The garage has a basement. That's where they made the stuff. The basement is all concrete with vents out the back of the garage that resemble the ones I've seen for dryers. The entrance to that room is under the junker car."

"Are your visits to the emergency room documented?" Beatrice asked.

"He took me to different hospitals. I've been to Lovelace, Presbyterian, and UNM, both here and in

Albuquerque. The neighbors were afraid of my father, so they didn't say anything. He has guns hidden all over the house. Things were okay until they started to use what they made. They were mean, but they didn't break any bones or threaten us with guns. If what I saw on TV was true, Mama and Papi were never good parents but Felipe and I didn't get hurt as much. You won't take me away from Hector and Steele because I told, will you?"

"No, your name will never come up. I'm going to do a more thorough search of your house, though, with dogs," Rivers assured Matteo. Both he and Sanchez shook their heads.

Beatrice sighed. "I'm sorry, Matteo. Your parents knew how to work the system and, as a result, the system failed you and your brother. I'll research the other hospitals and show your picture to the staff. They'll remember and pick out your records, even if they were filed under a different name."

"What can you do, Beatrice, so that they never have to go back?" Steele asked.

"After Hector called me this morning, I asked for and received a restraining order keeping the parents away from the kids. I have asked Judge Anderson for an emergency order awarding temporary custody of both boys to you and Hector until we finish our investigation pending your certification. I received your paperwork from LA this morning, Agent Steele. Agent Rivers, I'd like a copy of your report. I don't want Matteo to have to be put in protective custody. If you get enough evidence, they'll go away for a long time, and, even if they refuse to terminate their parental rights, they won't get out until the boys are both of age."

"Why can't we get more than temporary

custody?" Steele asked with heat.

"CYFD has to investigate to determine if the boys have any living relatives who want them. After that, we have to clear you. Hector was already approved as a foster parent here in New Mexico, but you weren't. Once we get that done, we can ask a judge, on the basis of the results of Agent Rivers and Agent Sanchez's investigation, to terminate the Penas' parental rights."

"What happens after that?" Steele got up to pace.

"Then you can apply for full custody and adoption. The process will probably take a year or more, but I won't let them be moved anywhere else while the wheels are turning." Beatrice wrote some notes in a folder.

"If they find relatives?" Steele asked.

"I don't have any relatives," Matteo interrupted. "Mama's brother died in a drug bust, and Papi didn't have any brothers or sisters. My grandparents are dead. I went to the funerals in Mexico, but Felipe and I are both citizens. We were born here."

"Are your parents citizens?" Rivers asked sharply.

"My mother has a green card, and my father was born here. Abuela went back to Mexico when Felipe was born. She died there last year. Can we please stay here?" Matteo begged Beatrice. "We had a cooked dinner last night and dessert with nuts and sprinkles. We had sheets and comforters on our beds. I didn't have to clean the bathroom before I let Felipe take a shower, and we have new pajamas. Steele even bought Felipe a new bear." Matteo started to sob.

"Don't worry. No one is going to take you away from us. I promise you that." Steele gave Beatrice and Rivers a withering stare.

Rivers stood. "I'm going to get my men to go back over the house. I'll keep the kids out of it." He walked to the door.

Beatrice Marks followed him out. "I'm going to go talk to the neighbors for further proof of abuse."

Steele handed Beatrice her coat. "Sanchez, could you stay a few moments while I see the others out."

Sanchez stayed behind and watched as Rivers and Beatrice left.

When he came back to the great room, he asked Sanchez, "How about a cup of coffee?"

"That would be good. I didn't get a chance to have one at the office." Sanchez wandered into the kitchen after him.

Matteo pulled on the bottom of Steele's shirt. "Do you have any chores for me?"

"Have you made your bed and put your dirty clothes in the hamper?" Steele asked.

"Yes, I did."

"Rivers brought over your schoolbooks. You should read ahead so you don't miss too much."

"Okay," Matteo said, resigned.

"Why the long face?" Steele asked.

"I have trouble at school because I can't see that well."

Steele's mouth went tight again. "Do you know your old doctor's name?" he asked gently.

"Dr. Burgess. He was at Lovelace, in the clinic."

"How long have you and Felipe been seeing him?"

"For as long as I can remember. He didn't ask too many questions, Papi said."

"I'll get Beatrice to pick up your records, and we'll see a new doctor and an eye doctor as soon as I can arrange it. In the meantime, try these." Steele pulled out a pair of Dollar Store reading glasses he kept for fine print.

"Okay, I'll try. I think I would do better at school if I could see," Matteo said in a forlorn voice.

"Then we'll take you to the doctor for regular glasses and you'll see, and we'll get you a tutor to catch up." He patted the boy on the back.

Matteo hugged him. "You and Hector are the best."

Steele's felt the heat as his face turned a bit red. He was embarrassed because he didn't feel like he had done anything more than any other man would who was confronted with the same situation, but he hugged Matteo back. Matteo went upstairs with his schoolbooks and the glasses.

"You're doing a good thing, Adams. I was there yesterday. The place was a pigsty. The only rooms that were tidy were the boys' rooms, and now I know it wasn't the mother who kept them clean." Sanchez spat out the words.

"I asked you to stay to ask if you wanted to spend Thanksgiving with Dare, Aden, Aden's mom, and our bunch. Thanksgiving is at Dare's. Christmas will be here, and you're also invited to Christmas dinner."

"Thanks for caring, Steele. I was pretty messed up when I came here from Denver. You've helped a lot. I consider you a friend. What can I bring?"

"For Dare and Aden's, nothing. Aden and his mother will have enough to feed the whole of Kirkland Air Force Base. For here, appetizers—the frozen ones at Costco or maybe cheese and crackers. I don't think I can manage to learn to make them from scratch with everything else there is to do this year." Steele laughed. "Hector and I are new at cooking. Aden and his mother will be here to make sure nothing goes terribly wrong."

"I'm already anticipating the food. Tell me what to get the kids," Sanchez said.

"They need everything. I'll give you clothing sizes, but call us if you decide to buy a toy. I don't want duplications. These kids have never had a Christmas. Hector and I are going all out. Matteo had to tell Felipe that he wasn't a bad boy, that the reason Santa didn't come was because he lost their address. I assured Felipe this morning that the FBI sent Santa their change of address so it wouldn't get lost again."

"Those bastards. That was good thinking on Matteo's part. Why don't you fill out the change of address form at the post office? You have to do that anyway. So fill out two for each boy and I'll put the FBI stamp on the duplicates and address them to Santa." Sanchez finished his coffee.

"That's a good idea. Then Felipe won't worry that there will be another glitch. Thanks, Jerry. I'll do that today."

"Maybe you can do me a favor in return. Is there any chance you know some other gay men? I've been to the local bars and come up empty."

"I think Rivers is gay. If you want, I'll ask him for Christmas. He's just transferred in from Oklahoma City. He's handsome but a bit on the grumpy side." Steele laughed. "That could be because he isn't getting laid. When he calls me to tell me what happened at Pena's house, I'll ask him if he wants to have dinner with us."

Steele heard the Explorer pull into the garage. "That's Hector," he told Sanchez. "I have to help put up Christmas lights. Thanksgiving is next week, and I want to turn them on for the kids Thanksgiving Day."

"I'll get going and check in with Rivers. I'll call

you if we find anything else. Those are good kids. I'll make sure Rivers does nothing to fuck this up for them."

"Thanks, Sanchez. Come over here at noon on Thanksgiving, and we'll leave from here. It's hard to find Dare's house in Placitas if you don't know the area." Steele walked with him to the front door.

Steele turned around to find Felipe barreling toward him, calling his and Matteo's name. Matteo came running down the stairs. "Is everything okay? Are you hurt?"

"I'm fine. You have to see what we got." Felipe giggled.

Steele watched Hector smile.

Felipe hugged Matteo. "Wait till you see. Hector bought a lit-up sled with a reindeer. A snowman and lights for all the bushes and trees. He got those icicle lights for the top of the house and *luminarias* for the walkways and stucco walls. We bought wooden slats to put up to outline the house and a lit-up Santa that moves his arms and legs for the roof."

Steele cocked an eyebrow at Hector.

Felipe's small frame danced with excitement. "Put on your coat," he told his brother. "Hector says we can help."

Matteo's eyes went to Steele to ask for permission.

"Go ahead, you can hit the books later today and I'll help." Matteo gave him a hug and went to the coat closet for his jacket.

Steele had a hard time controlling his anger. He was glad Hector wasn't there for most of his discussion with Rivers, Sanchez, and Beatrice. He would have blown. These boys were starved for attention and affection. He saw a lot of hugs and kisses in his future. It was a nice thought.

Steele went outside to see what Hector brought home. Besides the lights, he'd bought hot chocolate with mini-marshmallows, apple cider with cinnamon sticks, and cookies.

Hector handed Steele a bag. "I ran into Mama at the store. Felipe was with me, and I told her about Matteo. She wants us there Christmas Eve. I told her I'd ask you."

"Whatever you want is fine with me." Steele put the few groceries away.

He reflected, "It's going to be a zoo. I'm the last of ten kids and there are eighteen grandchildren. With Matteo and Felipe, that makes twenty. I usually skip the party because my brothers and father don't support my 'lifestyle,' as they put it. They put up with me because I'm family, but that's about it. My father and brothers still don't get that it isn't a choice."

"How about this? Tell your mother we'll see her the day after Christmas for lunch and we'll bring the kids with us, that way they can meet the boys and there will be no embarrassing situations. Especially since Matteo is also gay," Steele suggested.

"That's a great idea. I start on nights the twenty-sixth, so we have an excuse to leave if things get hairy. Then we can trim the tree on Christmas Eve. We'll buy the tree the week before, stick it outside in a bucket of water, and put the lights on a couple of days before we trim it," Hector decided.

"Do they have the kind of trees you can plant afterward?" Steele asked. "We could plant it to commemorate the boys' first Christmas, our first Christmas together as a family."

Hector's eyes got a little misty. He turned away and said, "That sounds like a plan."

They spent the afternoon putting up the lights. Just as it started to get cold, Hector went inside. Fifteen minutes later, as Steele set the last *luminarias* on the walkway, Hector called out from the door, "Who wants cocoa or cider with cookies?"

Felipe jumped up and down, raising his hand. "Me, me."

"What about you, Matteo?" Steele asked.

"Yes, please." He grinned.

Hector smiled at Steele. "I floured some cube steak to make chicken-fried steak and put potatoes on boil for mashed potatoes. I'm going to open a can of peas. Steele, you can make the gravy; you're better at it than I am. We also have leftover salad. Boys, don't eat more than two cookies each so you have room for supper. You can have more cookies after dinner. The food will be ready by six."

The boys chatted happily during the meal and helped to clear. They took more cookies and cocoa up to their rooms to watch TV, leaving Hector and Steele alone for the first time since early that morning.

Steele poured coffee for himself. They sat down, and he filled Hector in on what Matteo told Rivers, Sanchez, and Beatrice. Hector sighed. "I knew the boys had it rough, but I had no idea how bad it was. That's why Matteo is such an old soul. I swear, it's a wonder the kid is still sane. Most adults couldn't have handled the shit they threw at him."

"He's still tentative, afraid that we'll throw them out. He desperately wants to stay here now that Felipe is with him. I want to see him being a kid, even if it means he's disobedient." Steele's voice was rough. He cleared his throat.

Hector shook his head. "I agree. I'd like to see him be selfish, even if it's only once."

Steele's cell phone rang. He read the name on the screen. "It's Rivers. I have to take this. I'll put him on speaker."

"Adams...."

"Adams, this is Rivers."

"You're on speaker. Gomez is with me." Steele spoke into the phone.

"That's good because the abuse isn't a federal case, it's local, and I want those bastards hung for everything you can get them on." Rivers sounded angry. His voice was hard enough to pound nails.

"That bad?" Steele asked. He couldn't imagine what could get Rivers so worked up. Generally, he was a pretty cool customer.

"We went over the house and found enough product to put them away for a very long time; long enough for Felipe to be an emancipated youth and attend college."

"Did you call Beatrice Marks?" Steele asked.

"Yeah, she's running a parallel investigation for abuse." Rivers coughed into the phone.

"You okay?"

"The stench in the basement under the garage was enough to give me ten migraines. It even got through the breathers. They didn't have enough ventilation. Eventually, it would have killed the kids in the house if the vents were closed. But we confiscated six kilos of heroin with a street value of $780,000, ten kilos of coke valued at $660,000, and ten kilos of methamphetamine, which is cheaper to make but has the same street value as coke, and some marijuana. The marijuana was obviously for personal use. The meth lab was put together so haphazardly they're lucky they didn't blow up the house with the kids in it, the bastards." There was disgust in Rivers' voice. And this stuff was in addition to what we already seized. These people were big time, puissant rather than pissant.

"With that kind of lab, could they have made all the meth you found there?" The law enforcement part of Steele's brain kicked in.

"No, it was transported into the house. They were trying to make additional money on the side. Maybe they were thinking of trying to cut the cartel out of the operation. With Matteo's information, we were able to pick up the whole crew. We missed half of them on the first raid." Rivers coughed again.

"Maybe you should see a doctor," Steel said, concerned.

"Nah, I'm okay. If Matteo hadn't said something, the others would have gotten away and the case against his parents wouldn't have been airtight. They had files stored in the lab, the fools. They thought they were keeping blackmail material against the cartel. Those files will actually convict all of them. The kids are safe. The judge remanded their parents with a bail of two million each, and I don't think the cartel isn't going to bail them out." Rivers sounded satisfied with his day's work.

"Rivers, change of subject. I know you're new to the area. We're having Christmas here. Would you like to come? This will be the kids' first real Christmas."

"Sure, thanks. Want can I bring?"

"Something cool for the kids, not expensive, just cool." Steele thought a moment. "Magic tricks or something like that."

"Sounds good to me. Sanchez coming?"

"Yeah." Steele was now curious why he asked.

"Sanchez is a good agent. Maybe he and I can go

in on something together. What time?" Rivers seemed anxious to come.

"Come sometime around two. That will give the kids time to play with their toys before we eat."

"Okay, I'll see you on Christmas. I'll call if anything new comes up in the case before then. It won't be a breach of protocol because your office was on the task force."

"I've got to put the kids to bed." Steele told him. *Rivers must be lonely. Sanchez will be good for him, and Jerry's a nice guy.*

"I won't keep you, then. Good night."

"Good night."

Chapter Seven

Thursday Evening

Hector came down the stairs. "The boys are in bed. I read Felipe and Matteo a story, kissed them both good night, and tucked them under the covers."

"There's so much they need...." Steele put on another pot of coffee. "We drink way too much of this stuff."

"They need things, physically, as well as emotionally. They both have to go to the eye doctor, the pediatrician, and the dentist in addition to a child psychologist. Matteo didn't lie; he can't see very well, and both boys are much too thin."

Hector placed his head on Steele's shoulder. "I'd kill those bastards if they were anywhere near me."

"We've taken on a lot." Steele wrapped his arms around the shorter Hector and pulled him close. "But I'm positive the two of us can handle it together. Go into the great room and sit down. I'll be there in a minute as soon as I pour the coffee."

Hector sat on the large leather sectional, took off his shoes, and put his feet up on the ottoman. Steele came into the room with two mugs of coffee and set them on the side table so he could sit down without spilling. He handed Hector his mug and grabbed his own.

"Come and sit next to me." Hector patted the seat. "We have barely had time to talk to each other all day." Steele scooted over on the couch and sat close to Hector.

They sat side by side, each lost in their own thoughts, drinking their coffee. Steele decided to take the bull by the horns. He put down his coffee then grabbed Hector behind the head and gave him a scorching kiss.

His tongue parted Hector's lips. "That's it, open for me, baby."

Hector pulled away. "Forget the coffee. Let's take this to the bedroom. We have boys."

Steele stood and laughed, pulling Hector up with him. "Lead on."

Hector grabbed him by the front of his shirt and dragged him into the bedroom, closing the door. They tumbled to the bed where Hector ran his hands through Steele's dirty-blond buzz cut. Hector's own chestnut locks were slightly longer. Steele grabbed at them.

"I'm not good with words, Gomez, but as I told you yesterday, I love you. I have for a while now. I'm glad you didn't throw me out when I moved into your bedroom." He stroked Hector's face.

"I've been sappy for you since you moved into the house. I should have said something, but I was afraid that I'd scare you away." Hector's chocolate eyes gazed into Steele's blue ones.

"You wouldn't have scared me away. Aden is right. What did he call us, two dorks? If it weren't for the boys, we'd still be playing head games." He ran his hands down Hector's back. Hector shivered then planted kisses along Steele's jawline.

"I was going to confront you. I made up my mind Tuesday morning." Hector bit on Steele's earlobe.

"Good thing I made a preemptive strike by moving down here." He kissed Hector until they had to separate to breathe. "I didn't think I had a chance with you. Aden was small and gorgeous. I'm over six foot, built like a football player, and ten years older than you are. I didn't think I was your type."

Hector laughed. "You grew on me, and I found out that I love to bottom as well as top. Who knew? The age difference means less than nothing. At thirty-six, I could be Matteo's and Felipe's father. But I only want to do that with you. We were meant to be a family. The boys are comfortable here. As for me, I trust you with my heart and our boys."

"Dork..." He licked Hector's bottom lip, and things began to heat up. "I was serious when I said I love you."

"I know," Hector whispered.

"How do you know?"

"Because I love you, too." Hector moved his head to Steele's belly and sank his mouth down around Steele's cock.

"Yes, that feels so good, baby." His hands pulled gently on Hector's chestnut hair.

Hector worked his mouth up and down Steele's shaft.

"Baby, I'm close...I was close before we started. I want to come inside of you." Hector's mouth left Steele's hard member. He crawled up Steele's body, reached into the nightstand drawer, and brought out a bottle of lube and a condom. He started to prepare himself.

"No, baby, let me do it." Steele took the lube from his hand. Making his way down the bed, he caressed Hector's butt cheeks. "I love your hard, tight body."

"And I love it when your body covers mine." Hector laughed and caressed Steele's head.

"You keep pulling at my hair. I should probably grow it out to give you something to hold when I suck you." Steele chuckled.

"I like laughing in bed with you." Hector grabbed Steele's hand and kissed it.

"I like it too, baby."

Steele rolled on the condom and took the lube pouring some onto his fingers. He pushed open Hector's cheeks and started moving slowly toward his opening, gradually stretching the muscle to take two fingers. He searched and found the spot he was seeking, rubbing Hector's prostate.

"I want you now; I'm ready." Hector wiggled down on Steele's fingers.

He removed his fingers and turned Hector on his back. "I want to see you when I take you this time because, this time, we both know we're making love to one another."

Hector drew up his legs, and Steele entered him, slowly. "Baby you're so tight. You make me feel so good."

Hector pushed up, and Steele bottomed out. "Move damn it," Hector cried pushing up again.

Steele pulled almost all the way out and then slammed in again. "Topping from the bottom, Hector?"

"Yes, move. I want to feel your balls slapping my ass." Steele started to take him with a hard, pounding rhythm. Both men were damp with sweat despite the room being cool.

"I'm close," Steele warned.

"Touch me and I'm with you."

Steele grabbed Hector's cock between them and started to jack him off.

"Stt...eele, I'm going to blow."

"Come on, baby. I'm right with you." Hector erupted over Steele's hand. One more stroke and Steele filled the condom. Steele wiped his hand on a towel they had put on the side of the bed. He removed his condom, tied it off, put it in the wastebasket, got up and fetched a damp cloth from the bathroom and cleaned himself and Hector then tenderly dried them both with the towel.

He got back into bed and pulled Hector back into his arms. "Tomorrow, we'll mingle the bank accounts and set a date for the wedding."

Hector, who had been half asleep, perked up. "Did you say wedding? You didn't ask me to—"

"Do I have to? We love each other; we've got two boys to raise. I assumed that marriage was the next logical step."

"A guy likes to be asked." Hector almost pouted.

"I told you, I'm not one for flowery words, but if you insist. Marry me, Hector. I love you and couldn't imagine my life without you."

"My romantic FBI Agent, not. But I'll take you." Hector turned and kissed Steele lightly on the lips. "Let's go to sleep. We'll talk more after we get the boys settled." He turned, nestled his butt between Steele's thighs, and fell asleep leaving Steele laughing.

Steele settled down, put his arms around Hector's waist, pulled him closer, and did just that.

Friday Morning

Hector kissed the sleeping Steele at six, showered, changed into a fresh uniform then came downstairs to make coffee for Steele and prepared to leave for his seven-to-three shift at the sheriff's office. White had called in sick, and someone had to work the shift. He found Matteo wrapping a bacon and egg sandwich on a hard roll along with filling a thermos of coffee for him to take to work.

"Matteo, what are you doing up so early?"

"I was making breakfast. It's one of my chores."

"Matteo, we haven't given you any chores yet, and I don't want you getting up to make breakfast for everyone. Either Steele or I will do that. I want you to get the proper amount of sleep. If you must do a chore, take out the trash to the garbage can in the garage after dinner, okay?"

"I'm sorry I made you angry at me."

"Son, I'm not angry. I want you to know that we don't require you to earn your keep here. We want to love you, provide for you, and keep you safe. Your jobs are to do well in school, make your bed, keep your room neat and, if you must, take out the garbage. You're not going to be thrown out and neither is Felipe."

"I heard voices." Steele came out of the bedroom in sleep pants and a Harvard T-shirt. He eyed Matteo. "You're supposed to be in bed."

Matteo's eyes went from Hector to Steele. "I'm not supposed to make breakfast?"

"Nope," Steele said.

"As I said, we'll do that," Hector reiterated. "Now, either go back to sleep or quietly watch TV in the bedroom, but don't wake up Felipe. He needs to

A.C. Katt

get more sleep, as do you. So, if you're not going back to sleep, lie on the bed and watch TV, but keep the volume low."

"I'll call you when breakfast is ready." Steele ruffled his hair.

"Thank you for making my breakfast, but this is something you don't have to do anymore unless you're helping Steele or me." Hector gave Matteo a kiss on top of his head and shooed him away.

Steele and Hector watched him go back upstairs. Hector said, "I'll call Beatrice today and get a recommendation for a child psychologist."

"I have to put the kids on my health insurance. I don't want them to have to depend solely on Medicaid." Hector shook his head.

"I'll put them on mine, too." Steele poured himself a cup of coffee.

"You have to wait until you're approved as a foster parent. Beatrice already put in the papers with Judge Anderson awarding us temporary custody. She also put in for guardianship and eventual adoption. But, yes, that would be a good thing to do once you are, then we wouldn't have to depend only on doctors that accept Medicaid. I'll tell Beatrice to put a rush on that. I've got to run, or I'll be late for my shift." Hector grabbed his keys.

"What can I do to help things along until you get home?" Steele put half and half and a teaspoon of sugar in his coffee. "

"The kids need physicals. Could you find us a pediatrician? Also, go on the net and start ordering stuff for Christmas. Read their list but don't limit yourself to it. They need everything. I want to research gaming systems and bicycles. I think Aden and Dare are getting them trains. Love you, honey, got to go."

***

Steele started peeling and cutting up potatoes, onions, and garlic for home fries and took out enough eggs to make three ham-and-cheese omelets. He heard steps on the stairs. Matteo stuck his nose around the corner.

"I know I can't help, but can I talk to you while you cook and watch what you do?" Matteo ducked his head. "I kind of like cooking."

"Can't sleep?" Steele took his potatoes off a boil and drained them in the colander.

"I never can once I get up, and there isn't anything for me on television," Matteo groused.

"Even with all those channels?" Steele chuckled.

"I didn't go through all of them. I guess I wanted company. I'm not used to having anyone to talk to but Felipe and you're...." Matteo sat on the stool at the kitchen counter, appearing to be a little embarrassed.

"I'm what?"

"Well, you and Hector are like me. I've never talked to anyone who.... About...you know...before."

"You mean about being gay. What do you want to know?" Steele squeezed Matteo some fresh orange juice in the juicer, gave him the juice, and sat down with his coffee, hoping that it wasn't time for the sex lecture.

"Did I do something that made me be this way?" Matteo asked fearfully.

"No, you were born gay. You didn't do anything that made you this way."

"But the priest says it's wrong." Matteo started to

cry. Steele grabbed onto him and stroked his hair.

"There is nothing wrong with you. Hector used to be Catholic. We go to the Episcopalian Church because they have no problem with gay people. Jesus never said anything bad about being gay. It was the men who ran the church who decided it was wrong, not God, and now the Supreme Court of the United States says that gay people can marry." Steele stood up and gave Matteo a hug and went to the stove, taking down the skillet from the pot rack.

"Are you and Hector married?" Matteo asked, clearly interested.

"Not yet, but I asked him, and he said yes." Steele started to crack open eggs. "Do you want American or cheddar cheese in your omelet with the ham?" Steele took out the cheddar for himself.

"I don't know what cheddar is. Can I taste a little of it?" Steel crumbled off a small piece and handed it to Matteo who put it on his tongue. "This is good. It has more flavor than American cheese. Felipe will like it, too."

"It's eight o'clock. Go upstairs, wash up, and get dressed. Have Felipe do the same. By the time you come back, the omelets and potatoes will be ready." Steele melted some butter and oil together in the skillet to fry up the potatoes. He cut up the ham and located the omelet pan in the cabinet under the stove.

Steele heard the shower start, turned the potatoes in the pan, and grated the cheese. He turned on the oven to warm then heard the boys on the stairs. "Set the table for three. Breakfast will be ready in ten minutes."

Matteo got the plates, and Felipe the silverware. Matteo also found the placemats and the paper napkins.

"This is nice, eating together," Felipe said. Matteo nodded in agreement.

"Most of the time we will eat together, unless Hector or I have to work."

Matteo smiled that big wide grin that Steele searched for when the boy was happy. There weren't too many of those. He had to get him to the psychologist.

The three of them sat at the kitchen table, eating omelets and home fries and drinking fresh juice. The boys had hot cocoa, and he had more coffee. The phone rang.

Steele glanced down at the Caller ID. "Hi, Hector."

"I talked to Beatrice. She has a release from CYFD to obtain the boy's medical records. I asked Dare and he recommended Dr. Lopez at the UNM Family Medicine Clinic. He got an emergency appointment for today at eleven. Can you take them?"

"Sure. We're having breakfast. I'll pick up the records from Burgess and bring them with me. What about Medicaid and insurance cards?"

"Beatrice called Lopez's office and faxed them the Medicaid cards and proof of identity. She also sent them papers designating me as the foster parent who has medical authorization to have them treated. I'll take an early lunch and meet you there."

"Okay. In the meantime, I'll do some grocery shopping with the boys. Since I'm off until after the holidays, I'll do the cooking," Steele offered.

Hector deadpanned, "You need the practice."

Steele rolled his eyes. "I'm also making an appointment with the eye doctor as soon as I can get one. Matteo needs glasses for school. He's using my reading glasses and they're too big."

"Call today. I told Beatrice we'd have them back in school after the Thanksgiving break. There is so much to do to get them straightened out before they go to a new school. Thank God we got them some clothes and winter coats."

"Okay, we'll meet you at UNM Sandoval's Clinic at ten forty-five."

Chapter Eight

Friday, Late Morning

Steele got the boys dressed and into the car. They went to Dr. Burgess's office and collected the boy's medical records. They arrived at Lopez's office at ten forty-five. Hector was already there, straightening out the paperwork.

The receptionist said, "Dr. Rourke spoke to Dr. Lopez. He wants to see the records before he sees the boys."

Steele handed her the records he obtained from Burgess' office. "There may be more. Both children were abused and probably have records at most of the local urgent care clinics as well as Loveless and Presbyterian."

The receptionist tsked and lifted her head, spotting the boys. "Poor kids." She gave the record to someone wearing a uniform, like a nurse or PA.

"We have them now. They'll do fine," Steele assured her. They waited about fifteen minutes.

A medical assistant came out to the waiting area. "Matteo and Felipe Pena?" she asked.

Hector and Steele stood up with the boys.

"Who is Sheriff Gomez?" Her eyes moved from Hector to Steele.

"I am, but my partner is applying to be the co-parent, so he has my permission to hear about the boy's physical condition."

"Come in, then." The boys, Hector, and Steele followed her into a treatment room. "Undress the boys completely, put them in these gowns, and the doctor will be in shortly."

Hector took Matteo, Steele, Felipe, and they stripped them down, putting on the examination gowns. The doctor arrived just as Steele snapped the last closure.

"I'm Dr. Lopez. I'll take Matteo first as he was recently hurt." The doctor examined him, checking his scrotum, ribs, and cheek. He followed up by thoroughly examining Felipe. "You can let them get dressed."

Steele and Hector both waited for the doctor to speak. The doctor began in a grim voice. Both boys are badly bruised, as you can see. Bruising is caused by a blow or impact rupturing underlying blood vessels. Frequent bruising is not good for the body. Matteo has cracked ribs and other remodeled bones according to the X-rays taken a few days ago in the ER. Neither boy has had his flu shot and both are missing some vaccinations. I'll give them their flu shots and vaccinations today. They need to eat. They're both underweight. They need meals with protein, plenty of vegetables, fruit, and good carbohydrates. I want them to take vitamins. Along with their vaccinations, I'm giving them a shot of B-12. Make sure their vitamins contain iron. Tell my receptionist to give them an appointment in four weeks and we'll check their progress."

Steele spoke up. "Matteo has a vision problem. He says his schoolbooks are blurry. I'm taking him to the eye doctor as soon as I can get an appointment."

The doctor made a note on the chart. "Have the eye doctor send me a report. Have Felipe's eyes checked, too."

The nurse brought in a tray with the flu shots, and the doctor took the vaccinations from a cabinet in the treatment room. The doctor gave the boys their immunizations and the vitamin shots. Felipe whimpered, but Matteo whispered something to him and he stopped.

"They can get dressed. I hope to see them gain a few pounds before the next visit. Don't go overboard on sweets; that's not a healthy way to gain weight. Having dessert at dinner is plenty of sugar—no sugared soda, candy, or junk food snacks. Make exceptions only for the holidays. Also watch the juice; some of the packaged stuff is pure sugar."

"We squeeze our own." Hector straightened Felipe's buttons.

"Good. Give them fruit, nuts, and cheese, sandwiches, muffins with fruits and nuts in them, and cut-up vegetables when they're hungry between meals. Whole wheat pasta has good complex carbs. Popcorn with butter and salt is also a good snack. Peanut butter, yogurt with fruit and granola, raisins, whole grain cereal—I'll have the nurse give you a list of recommended food and snacks for young boys. They also need to see a dentist."

"Thank you, Doctor. When the boys come in, Steele or I will always be with them, no one else. Their parents are up on charges of abuse and neglect of the children from the state and drug trafficking from the federal government. We want permanent custody and to adopt both boys." Hector paced.

"Well, I'll put in a good word for you. From what I read in Burgess' records, you are seeking to rectify years of neglect. I have no idea why he didn't report the parents." Steele shook the doctor's hand.

He kissed Hector. "We brought you lunch because, otherwise, you wouldn't eat. I made a ham, prosciutto, pepperoni, and provolone sub, wet, just how you like it. It's in the plastic bag with a bag of chips and an apple. Take it back to the office. The boys and I are going to Whataburger for lunch and then to the grocery store."

"Be careful. They may still get out on bail," Hector whispered.

"I have my weapon," Steele said grimly.

"Good." Hector nodded his head.

Friday Afternoon

Steele called from his Navigator and managed to get an appointment with the eye doctor for both boys on Saturday. The doctor had cancelations, so Steele was able to get them in to see the doctor by shamelessly dropping Dare's name. He pulled out of the parking space, and he and the boys headed for the grocery store.

Mindful of what the doctor said, when Matteo brought him a sugared cereal, he said no. "Wouldn't you rather have pancakes, eggs, cinnamon toast, French toast, and waffles for breakfast?"

"What if you can't make our breakfast? Can I make Felipe eggs if you or Hector can't?" Matteo persisted. Steele knew this was because the boys had gone hungry before Matteo learned to cook a few basic dishes.

"If we're not around, and you don't have a babysitter, you may cook eggs, but nothing else unless you're helping Hector or me. Does that make you feel better?" Steele ruffled his hair.

Matteo considered what Steele said and nodded his head.

Steele put lots of red meat and chicken in the cart, along with pork chops, ribs, bacon and ham. "What kind of vegetables do you like?" he asked both boys.

"Peas, carrots, green beans, corn, and potatoes. Don't know of any others. Those were the ones that came with the frozen dinners." Matteo shrugged.

Steele took the cart through the produce aisle and picked up Brussels sprouts, broccoli, spinach, and cauliflower. In the dairy aisle, he picked up cream cheese and sour cream to make a dill and onion vegetable dip to encourage the boys to eat vegetables. He bought Baby Bell cheese packaged in snack-size bites and dried fruit.

He put apples, pears, and mandarin oranges in the cart. Upon further consideration, he bought a large box of Honey Nut Cheerios; it wouldn't hurt for them to have cereal occasionally. He had a full cart at the checkout line. Matteo helped him unload the cart and bag the groceries, tying the tops of the plastic bags so the groceries didn't fall out in the trunk.

Steele's phone rang. It was Hector. "Keep the kids inside. Beatrice called. They made bail. Where are you?"

"I'm loading the car at the Albertson's parking lot."

"Shit, stay in the car until I can get Garcia over there to escort you home. He's two minutes out."

Hector sounded frantic. "When you get home, lock the garage and stay inside. Bolt all the doors and keep the kids with you in the great room. They shouldn't be able to get over the wall. I'll be home in ten minutes."

Steele heard the sirens and saw Garcia pull up. Garcia got out of the squad car. "Follow me, Adams. The father made threats against Matteo. Hector and I will update you at the house." Garcia turned on the lights and the sirens and led Steele and the boys home.

Steele opened the garage door, pulled his Navigator inside then locked the garage. He let Garcia in by the side door, and they secured it and threw the deadbolt. Garcia and the boys helped bring in the bags from Albertsons. After putting away the groceries and settling the boys in the great room, Steele put on a pot of coffee. Garcia set his weapon on the table, and Steele unstrapped his Glock and placed it next to Garcia's.

Steele had just finished pouring Garcia a cup of coffee when Hector ran into the house.

Steele raised an eyebrow. "What happened to set you off?"

"They made bail and went to CYFD and threatened Beatrice with a gun, vowing to find Felipe and Matteo and kill Matteo for giving them up. Beatrice called us right away."

"Threatening a witness is a crime. Can't you arrest them?" Felipe picked up his head.

"Calm down." Steele nodded at the boys watching TV in the great room.

Hector continued in a lower voice. "To arrest them, we have to find them. We've notified the Rio Rancho Police, the Albuquerque police, and the

Bernalillo Sheriff's Department. It would be a good idea to call Sanchez and Rivers. Their case depends in part on Matteo's information."

Steele stood and took his phone to the second bedroom on the ground floor that he and Hector used as a home office. He tapped in River's number.

"Rivers...."

"Adams here. Manny Pena and his wife are out on bail. The went to CYFD and threatened Beatrice Marks' life if she didn't tell them where the boys were. She didn't say and the security guard came out with his gun, so they ran off. Manny knows Matteo gave you information." Steele waited to see what Rivers would say.

"I'll call Sanchez, and we'll get some agents over there. We don't need to go for subtlety. We're there to protect those boys, you, and Hector. I assume Hector already brought a deputy in."

"Year, Edwards is here."

"Keep him there. Let me speak to Hector."

"Just a minute." Steele came out of the office and handed Hector the phone.

Hector went into the office, spoke for a few minutes, and hung up on his way back into the kitchen.

"We're supposed to stay here until they pick them up." Hector sighed. "I'm glad I got the lights done. Garcia, watch the front of the house. I'll call Abbott and Edwards to tell them what's going on. Rivers and Sanchez are sending over a few agents." Hector poured himself some coffee.

"Won't all the security draw attention to us?" Steele, the veteran of many stakeouts, was concerned.

"Yes, and this guy is bat-shit crazy enough to try to do something even with the agents here. He pulled a gun on Beatrice. Aren't the kids supposed to go to the eye doctor tomorrow?" Hector gave Steele a kiss on the cheek and sat at the table with him and Garcia.

"Yeah, how are we going to do that? I don't want to cancel that appointment. We'll have to wait a month for another, but we can't put the kids in danger." Steele's face turned hard. "Even after we got the kids away from them, they're still fucking up their lives."

"The Sheriff's Department will escort them. You're going to the eye doctor in Bernalillo, aren't you?"

Steele nodded.

"The Eyeglass Store is in Sandoval County and therefore my jurisdiction. Garcia and Edwards can escort us, and both of us will go armed."

"The appointments will take two hours. We have to bring something to amuse the boys. Garcia, you have kids. If I give you some money, can you go to Walmart and get two of those handheld games?"

"Sure, my kids are that age. I know what to get. When this mess is done, we live a few blocks over. The kids will be going to school together. It would be good for Matteo and Felipe to have friends."

"Thanks, Garcia. Let me get my wallet." Steele went into the bedroom and got his wallet from the dresser. He pulled out five hundred dollars. "Will this be enough?"

"Yeah. I'll get them Gameboys, mid-priced, proven technology, and plenty of games. I'll pick up some games appropriate for the boys' ages. I can go as soon as Rivers' DEA Agents and your FBI guys arrive."

Steele turned toward Hector. "Will he come at us in the daylight?"

"By now, he's high on meth and crazy. What do you think?" Hector narrowed his eyes.

"Don't get annoyed. I wanted your professional assessment of the situation. I value your input," Steele soothed

"I'm sorry I snapped. I'm worried about the kids." His eyes went to Steele

"I know. We'll get through this. Garcia, when the agents arrive, tell them I have fried pork chops for dinner along with mashed potatoes and corn on the cob."

"Are you sure we have enough?" Hector asked. "I can go get Church's Chicken."

"We have enough. I bought three packages of pork chops. They were on sale. We have plenty of potatoes, and I'll give the boys the corn and open a couple of packages of frozen green beans. I also bought a huge jar of applesauce." Steele shrugged.

Hector chuckled and said to Garcia, "Steele has strange buying habits. He buys the biggest jar in the store, says the cost per serving is less. I maintain it doesn't matter if it gets thrown out, but now that we have two growing kids, he's absolved."

Steele glanced up at the clock. It was two. The boys had hamburgers at noon. It was time for a snack. He walked into the great room. "Who wants some of that banana bread we bought?" Happy faces nodded. "Come into the kitchen and we'll get you a slice with a glass of milk."

The boys got up and were running into the kitchen when a shot rang out, breaking the glass in the back door.

"Hit the floor!" Steele yelled.

Felipe started to cry. "Matteo's bleeding."

Hector used his radio. "Get me a bus, now."

Hector crawled to Matteo.

Matteo whispered, "Felipe?"

"He's okay, son." Hector turned Matteo over and put pressure on a wound in his arm.

Steele called Rivers. "Where the fuck are you? Matteo's been shot."

"We have the parents in custody. We caught them trying to get away."

"Not fucking good enough." Steele heard the sirens. He unlocked the door, picking up a hysterical Felipe in his arms. "In the great room," he told the EMT.

The EMT wrapped Matteo's arm. "Which hospital?"

"UNM, Sandoval. We'll follow in the Navigator." Steele got in the driver's seat. Hector got in the back to hold the still-crying Felipe. He buckled him into the booster seat they'd bought and kissed his hair, murmuring reassurance that Matteo would be all right.

"It was Papi and Mama. I saw them through the window. I didn't have time to say anything before the gun hit Matteo. It's my fault."

Hector rocked him in his arms. "No, chipmunk, it's not your fault. Your father and mother did this and, if I have my way, they're going to be buried in a hole so deep it will take their whole lives just to make it down to the bottom."

Chapter Nine

Friday, Late Afternoon/Early Evening

Hector handed Felipe to Steele and followed Matteo into a treatment room. After a few minutes, Beatrice Marks came running into the ER. "Where is Matteo?"

Steele sat in the waiting room with Felipe on his lap, the boy's head resting on his shoulder, where he was crying softly. "He's in the treatment room. The bullet hit his arm. It went straight through. He had turned to grab Felipe's hand. If he hadn't, the bullet would have hit his heart."

"Where did that bastard get a gun? He had one in my office. I thought the DEA and the FBI took all of the guns from his home," Beatrice said, her anger evident.

"They found all of Pena's guns except the nine millimeter he had taped under his vehicle. He bragged to Sanchez that they didn't find it. He shot Matteo and threatened you with that."

"How did they know where he was?" Beatrice asked in frustration.

"The day he abused Matteo on the lawn, the wife

said no one would take a gay teen. Hector told her he would take him. Pena found out that he was the sheriff and had someone follow him home."

Beatrice sat down heavily on the chair next to Steele. "This should be enough." She was shaking.

"Enough for what?" Steele rubbed circles on Felipe's back. He wasn't sobbing anymore, but his eyes still leaked tears.

"Enough to start the process to permanently terminate their parental rights. Was she with him?"

"Felipe saw both of them. He's upset because he thinks he didn't say something quick enough."

Felipe picked up his head. "I saw them. Both of them. Mama put her finger to her lips to tell me to be quiet. I was about to scream, and then it happened." Felipe started to sob again.

"Rivers got their bail revoked. The ball's in your court, Beatrice. Do something so these boys never have to think about those bastards again," Steele hissed.

"It takes at least six months to terminate their rights, but I can guarantee you custody until then."

"What do you mean 'until then'?"

"If one of them goes through rehab and does good time, they could reapply for custody of the kids. We'd fight it, but it's possible the court will put them back with their family once they've done their time."

Steele's expression turned to stone. "Beatrice, if you value your job, you will make absolutely sure these kids never see those people again unless it's in a court where they are surrounded by police."

"I'll try my best, Mr. Adams, but I have to follow the law and the direction of the court." Beatrice's answer made Steele scowl.

Hector came out to the waiting room. "It nicked

a bone but went through his arm. They're going to go back to the house. The bullet is probably in the furniture, rug, or wall. Then they're sending in crime scene cleanup. They'll be done by the time we get out of here."

"Can Felipe and I see Matteo?" Steele asked, somewhat impatient.

"I came out to get you. Matteo is worried about his brother."

Steele, Hector, and Felipe walked back to the treatment area. Matteo was sitting up on the gurney with a bandage on his upper left arm. Felipe threw himself on his brother. "I was so worried. I saw them but didn't have time to scream." He started to sniffle again.

"I'm okay. You didn't do anything wrong. We're all going home for fried pork chops. Hector promised."

"Matteo's okay? He can come home with us?"

"He's okay, chipmunk." Hector smiled and ruffled Felipe's hair.

"Why do you call Felipe, chipmunk?" Matteo asked, puzzled.

"Because he chatters like one." Hector chuckled.

A big smile broke out on Matteo's face. "You're right, he does. I can call him Chip."

"I'd rather have that name than the one they gave me." Felipe said, a mulish expression on his face.

Matteo grabbed his brother and hugged him. "I'll make it all right, you'll see."

"I don't want to go back. They'll hurt me worse."

"I know, I know." Matteo patted Felipe on the back.

"Let's go make pork chops. The doctor has

released you. You'll have some pain, but no lasting damage aside from a scar." Hector brought over Matteo's clothing.

Steele spied the clothing and then lifted his eyebrow to Hector. "Garcia and Edwards went to the house." Steele nodded his head.

There was a commotion in the hall. "There's the devil's spawn who got his own father shot up, little faggot, and now he's going to turn his brother into one."

Felipe ran out of the room before Steele or Hector could catch him. "You stop calling Matteo names. I spit on you. You are not my Papi. I live with Hector and Steele now, and I never have to see you again."

"We'll see about that, little man, we'll see." He grabbed Felipe with the arm that wasn't cuffed to the deputy.

Steele left Matteo's room. "If you don't want to be dragged off to federal prison, I'd let go if I were you. Witness tampering is a federal offense and can give you a lot of time to contemplate your sins in a federal penitentiary."

Manny let go of Felipe. "Take the little traitor, then. But remember, Felipe, and tell your faggot brother, payback is a bitch." The guards took him away.

Felipe turned to Steele. "I'm not ever going back. I don't care what happens. I'm not leaving my brother."

"I'll make sure you don't have to, chipmunk." Steele hoisted him up in his strong arms and carried him back to Hector and Matteo.

Matteo was upset. "How many times have I told you not to go near him when he's high? Shit, you shouldn't be going near him at all." Matteo put his hand over his mouth and mumbled, "Sorry, Hector."

"Someone is clearing the table by himself." Hector appeared stern. "I told you that cursing would bring more chores."

"I'll help. Matteo's hurt." Felipe snuggled nearer to his brother.

"Tonight, we'll all help, but next week, one day, Matteo cleans by himself for cursing." Felipe gave Hector the stink eye.

"He's right. I did curse, and I was warned. Clearing the table is no big deal, and I'll remember not to curse again. Apologize to Hector."

"I'm sorry...." Felipe said in a small voice. Hector gave Felipe a hug.

"You're forgiven. Now get dressed, son. We're going home for supper."

Hector signed the discharge papers and received instructions on care of the wound, and the four of them got into the car to go home. The phone rang in the Navigator. Steele said, "Hello, you're on speaker."

"It's Dare. Is the kid okay? Edwards called."

"A flesh wound in the upper arm, but if he hadn't turned to help his brother, it would have hit his heart." Steele spoke, still feeling the tension.

"Not something I'd want on my OR table. Thank God he dodged the bullet, literally. Will you still be able to come on Thursday?"

"We're going home now. He'll be fine," Steele reassured both Dare and, by proximity, Felipe.

"I have to introduce them to Debra. She's pouting because she doesn't have any grandchildren yet," Dare told them.

"The boys meeting Debra would be a good thing. They need a female role model, too. When you finally decide to have them, we can give you some tips on raising kids. We're pulling into the driveway, and I promised fried pork chops." Steele put the Navigator into park and pushed the button to turn off the engine. He closed the garage door. "I'm ready to go into the house, Dare."

"Go make your pork chops. We'll see you Thursday. We're not dressing up, so the boys can come in jeans and sweaters."

"I'm taking them shopping for clothing on Sunday. They'll have a nice pair of slacks and an oxford shirt, tie, and a pullover. They need to learn to dress well when it's appropriate. I'm in the garage. We'll see you Thursday."

As they entered the kitchen , he heard Felipe whisper to Matteo, "Do you think that they'll find us to be too much trouble and give us back?"

Hector turned his head to see the boys in the backseat. "Never think that you are too much trouble. Steele and I can handle anything your parents throw at us. Get it straight. We want you in our home and our lives. You're our family. Sometimes, the families you make are better than the one you're born with."

Matteo put his finger on the top of his bandage. "That's the truth," he muttered.

Saturday Morning

The next morning, they headed to the eye doctor. "We're getting the examination here, but we're taking our prescription and going to the eyeglass store at the mall so the glasses will be done in an hour," Hector told the kids.

It was no surprise that Matteo needed glasses,

but Felipe needed them, too. After an extensive examination, they went to the mall, and Steele and Hector helped them pick out some nice, reasonably priced frames. Steele was examining frames when Hector tapped him on the shoulder. "The glasses are covered by the kid's Medicaid. Let's buy some clothes for them to wear to Aden and Dare's. That way we can go out for tree decorations this week without having to worry about clothes shopping. We have plenty left for Christmas. We're well under budget."

"Sounds good. The glasses won't be ready for an hour yet."

"Let's go to Macy's. The boys should each have one nice outfit that isn't jeans and a graphic T-shirt," Steele agreed.

Hector took them to the boy's department at Macy's. "Find nice pants, a buttoned long-sleeved shirt, and a sweater that goes over the shirt," he instructed then he let them loose.

"Are you sure you should have done that. Who knows what they will come up with?" Steele raised a brow.

"They have to learn but also to develop their own taste. We'll have the power of the veto." Hector turned his head around and spotted the boys over by the dress shirts. "See? I don't think Matteo is steering them wrong."

A half hour later, the boys came to them, holding clothes. Matteo had apparently helped his brother. He'd found two white button-down shirts, two light woolen sweaters—one red, one green, and two pairs of light wool slacks in charcoal gray. Every item was marked down. Obviously, Matteo did their clothes shopping.

Hector told the boys, "Try the pants on then we'll

go for shoes and decent athletic shoes. You'll also need white undershirts to wear under the dress shirts, and dress socks and ties."

The boys tried the clothing on and the fit, even the length of the slacks, was perfect on both of them. "I picked out the stuff that was on sale, but this stuff is still pretty expensive. Are you sure you don't want to go to Walmart?" Matteo asked Steele.

"No, no Walmart for clothes and shoes. I went there the first night because it was an emergency situation. We want you to have well-made clothing that won't wear out before you outgrow it."

They went for shoes next, staying at Macy's for dress shoes and then heading to the sneaker store where Steele bought them two pairs of Nike Air Max. "You don't have to spend that much money on sneakers for both of us. I'll wear the ones you got me from Walmart." The clerk measured Matteo's foot. Matteo and Felipe were in awe when they tried on the sneakers.

Hector watched the boys. He could read the longing on their faces. He called the clerk. "They'll wear them home." Both boys' eyes popped with surprise and joy.

"Let's go to Rudy's and get barbecue for lunch. We can have leftovers for dinner. We have both spaghetti and pork chops." Hector took the bag containing Felipe's old shoes. "Do you want your old sneakers?"

"Do you want me to keep them?" Felipe's voice trembled.

"Not unless you want to keep them." Felipe shook his head.

Hector headed to one of the huge trash receptacles in the food court and dumped Felipe's pair of beat up, holey sneakers in it.

Monday Morning

Steele began the process of qualifying as a foster parent by taking classes in parenting. Beatrice said, even though Hector qualified already, she had to do another home visit to qualify Steele. Steele was walking in the door from his class as Beatrice was leaving.

"Onerous?" She smiled.

"No, just plain common sense, and, remember, I took the classes in L.A. How long does this take?"

"Normally, about four to six months. The kids are here now because they were placed here on an emergency basis. It helped that you were licensed in California. Since I won't be able to place Matteo anywhere else but in a group home and he should be with his sibling, they can stay here for the time being, but you have to go through the process. Since you are an FBI agent, the background check will be easier. I've been here the required number of times for home visits."

"I'm off until after New Year. What else do I need to do?"

"You'll need a physical. We have the background check and references. I think I can pare four months down to two in this case." Beatrice walked toward the door. "It isn't often that I feel so good about a foster placement. I'll pull strings to make it happen as fast as I can. Finish the classes."

"I'll take two a day until I've met the requirement. I don't want Matteo and Felipe going anywhere else now that they are settling in here. I'll move out until I qualify as long as the kids can stay with Hector."

"That won't be necessary. As I said, this is an emergency placement, and Hector is fully qualified."

"I love those kids and don't want any harm to come to them because I didn't dot my Is or cross my Ts."

Beatrice patted Steele on the shoulder. "Don't worry. No judge in their right mind would give the kids back to those two even if it is state policy to try to reunite families."

"I sincerely hope not. Let me know, if push comes to shove. I meant it. I'll leave if I become a problem and move back in once I'm qualified."

"Like I said, not necessary." Beatrice saw herself out the door.

"I hope not," Steele muttered.

Chapter Ten

Late Tuesday Afternoon/Early Evening

Hector came back from work and immediately locked up his gun. The boys gave kisses and so did Steele, who had a cup of coffee waiting for him.

"I took the kids to the psychologist today with your prior authorization. She said Matteo has serious self-esteem issues and Felipe is always afraid unless he's near Matteo. Both kids have been physically and emotionally abused and may have PTSD; thus Felipe's night terrors. Matteo was on the verge of nervous collapse, worrying about his brother. She thinks our approach of just letting them be kids is the right path to take, but she wants to see them once a week."

"We'll take turns bringing them. I'll get my schedule and coordinate it with yours." Hector brought up the calendar application on his phone.

"Dr. Morris isn't putting them on medication. The doctor wants to see if a more wholesome environment and counseling can help since the PTSD was caught early. Obviously, Matteo has more issues than Felipe. He was with them longer and tried to protect his younger brother." Steele sat down with his own coffee while the boys watched TV in the great room.

"We'll have to schedule a private session where we can ask her what's best for the boys." Hector sipped from his mug.

"Debra wants to meet the boys. She thinks they need to experience making Christmas cookies. What do you think?" Steele asked.

"If she meets them on Thanksgiving and they get along, that's a great idea. It will give us time to shop and wrap. Even if we order from Amazon, we still have to wrap everything."

Steele considered what Hector said. "Yeah. We have to find a place to put the gifts so they don't snoop," Steele said. "Matteo is of the age when snooping begins."

"There is a crawl space over the garage that I floored with plywood, just in case. I think *just in case* has arrived."

"I'm curious, and I have to ask you this. Why such a big house? Five bedrooms, or four and an office, is pretty large for one man." Steele regarded him quizzically.

"It was a bargain during the housing crises. Besides, I always knew I wanted a family. That's why I applied to be a foster parent. You, *mí corazón*, were the icing on the cake. We have enough room for them to have a playroom and us to have an office." Hector leaned over and kissed Steele behind his ear.

"Makes sense, I guess. All I ever wanted was someone to love who loved me back." Steele stood and pulled Hector up into his arms.

"I love you back, honey. Why would I put up with

you for six months if I didn't?" Hector teased. Steele smacked his ass, and Hector squelched an ow.

"You can't do that, or the kids will think we beat on each other." Hector pretended to pout.

"But it's such a nice, round, tight ass. Perfect for an occasional swat." He rubbed his hand over where he'd smacked Hector.

"With their background, the kids won't view it as play," Hector reminded him.

Steele thought about that for a moment then said, "You're right. I'm going to kiss you instead."

"None of that now. We have boys to feed and some online shopping to do. I'm a Prime member at Amazon and get free shipping, so I'd prefer to order from them. I order from them for the nieces and nephews and have their presents delivered directly to their homes. It's better than braving the stores. I have this down to a science." Hector puffed up with pride.

"They need bicycles and computers, a gaming system and some games, and two handheld gaming systems. Garcia didn't get them because of the shooting, and Matteo needs a phone. We might have to get one for Felipe so Matteo can check in on him. He worries so much about his brother," Steele said on reflection.

"They need all sorts of clothing. I had you buy the clothing from Walmart as a throwaway. I want them better dressed than that. My sisters shop at JC Penny's, Burlington, and Target. Their clothing is more durable than Walmart's but not as expensive as Macy's. They need coats, hats, and gloves. A warm jacket and a lighter one, sweaters, sweatshirts, long-sleeved shirts, and jeans. The pajamas, robes, and slippers we picked up at Walmart will do for the time being." Hector made a few notes on the pad he carried in his pocket.

"I don't think we should buy bicycles, sight unseen. There are two bike stores in Corrales. I can go out early tomorrow morning because you're off the rest of the week and see what they have on display. If we still want to buy from Amazon, we'll have an idea what to order. The rest of the toys, we can point and click, but we have to buy the clothes so they are returnable in case the boys don't like them or they don't fit." Steele opened the refrigerator to get out the things for dinner.

"I saw beanbag chairs for the playroom that we can have personalized with their names. They have a TV in the playroom but need a music player with a docking station and speakers. Both boys also need headphones."

"The Samsung phones are readers, music players, alarm clocks, calendars, and phones. We have Wi-Fi in the house; they can text and send all the pictures they want from the house for free. I can put all four of us on my Verizon plan, but we'll have to buy the phones which aren't cheap. You're on Verizon, too. We can combine all four of us and save money." Steele pulled some oil out from under the cabinet and poured it in a saucepan. They were having hamburgers, French fries, salad, and tomato soup.

"We have to buy one of those mini fryers." Hector took the meat and began to form patties while Steele chopped onions and mushrooms.

"I'll put one on your list for Santa," Steele teased.

"A simpler phone plus a Kindle Fire might be a better idea than such an expensive phone. It does audio books, the Internet, and it's a reader." Hector rifled through Amazon on his laptop.

"You might be right. Maybe I'll get you the Samsung phone." Steele laughed.

"Seriously, we have to get some things for each other and from the boys, or Felipe will think Santa forgot us." Hector frowned.

"Make a list of small stuff that you need and were going to buy yourself, and I'll do the same. We can take the boys out and work from that. We've also got to tell them that Santa only comes to kids." Steele began to fry the mushrooms and onions in butter.

"When you get that physical, make sure they check your cholesterol. We eat too much fried food and butter. We've got to start to make healthier choices. We're parents now." Hector began cutting up greens for the salad.

"I'd like to go for the tree after supper. I want to get one before they are all picked over. While you were working today, the boys and I went online and found three nurseries that sell live trees, but you can only keep them indoors for five days after Christmas, or they come out of their dormant stage, and then, when we plant it, it will die. Also, we can't put a lot of lights on it," Steele explained.

"Maybe we should get a regular tree, but a really tall one. The boys would love that." Steele put the fries on paper towels to absorb the grease.

"While I'm out, I'll scout trees. I called to check in at the office, and Abbott said the best place for a large tree is Jeff's on Paseo del Norte. We can get a ten to fourteen footer there. The ceiling in the great room is fourteen feet."

"Fourteen would be too high; it wouldn't leave room for the star. Eleven to thirteen will do nicely, but be prepared to pay two to three hundred dollars for a good tree." Hector put the salad in the fridge.

"New Mexico doesn't have too many Christmas tree farms. You really should wait until a week before Christmas; otherwise, we'll be cleaning up needles on Christmas Day."

Steele blushed. "I've never had a live tree. My family had an expensive artificial tree, but I want a live one for the boys."

"Tell you what. After dinner, let's go and pick up lights at Costco. I like lots of lights. I generally like white lights, but, with the boys, we'll need some colored strands. LED lights are the way to go. They are energy efficient." Hector opened the can of soup and got out some milk.

"Getting energy efficient lights is an excellent way to teach the kids about conservation. That's a good idea. What do we do about decorations?" Steele put the patties on the grill attachment for the stove.

"We can go to the Christmas store in Old Town to get some special decorations, one for each of us, and we'll buy some more at Target and Costco." Hector stirred the soup and blew in Steele's ear. Steele's cock rose.

"Don't do that when we can't follow through. Tonight, I'm going to torment the hell out of you," Steele hissed.

"We'll see who torments who...." Hector gave him an evil smile.

Steele removed the buns from the grill and the last of the French fries from the saucepan with a slotted spoon. He called, "Matteo, Felipe, go wash up. Dinner's ready. Hurry up because we're going out after dinner."

Hector served the boys their soup and salad first. Matteo stared at Hector. Steele was at the stove flipping burgers. "Felipe and I were talking. Since we're going to stay here, both of you are going to be our dads. Can we call you Dad and Papa?"

Hector took a deep breath, and Steele stood stock still. Steele recovered first but kept his back to the boys, wiping at his eyes. "Are you sure?"

"Yep. We discussed it, and that man shouldn't be anyone's Papi, nor that woman anyone's Mama. We're sure."

Steele turned. Hector spied the moisture in his eyes.

Hector nodded. "Sure, we'd be honored."

Felipe looked up from his soup. "Thank you, Papa," he told Hector. Thank you, Dad." He and Matteo got up from the table and gave each of them a kiss and a hug."

Felipe whispered to Matteo, "See? I told you it would be okay."

The boys finished their soup and salad, and Steele served the burgers and fries. Matteo ate two burgers and Felipe one and a half.

"I'm glad to see you guys eating. You need to bulk up and get strong. Did you take your vitamins this morning?" Hector smiled at Felipe's milk mustache.

"Dad gave them to us with breakfast. They're gummy vitamins, not pills. They're fun to take. Dad made sure that Felipe knew they weren't candy and put them on a shelf he couldn't reach over the refrigerator. I'm finished. May I be excused so I can go to wash us up before we go out? We've got greasy fingers."

"Go ahead," Steele told them. "Papa and I will clean up. We'll be ready in fifteen minutes. Turn off the TV and all but one light in the great room. Get your coats, hat, and gloves. It's chilly outside."

The boys left the room. Steele gazed at Hector. "We are so lucky."

"Yes, we are." Hector smiled and kissed his partner lightly on the lips.

"I want to get them a dog for Christmas. We can get an older puppy, and the boys can take the dog with us to obedience class. It will give the boys a sense of responsibility." Steele waited to see what Hector would say.

"We'll get chewed shoes and dog crap on the rug." Hector shook his head. "You're right. Boys need a dog, but I'm not getting them a mutt. I want to know what to expect. We'll research breeds together and search for dogs without the boys. We don't need them to fall in love with a Great Dane."

Steele cracked up. "Or even worse, one of those yippy dogs with more hair than sense. I think a medium sized dog, intelligent and good with kids."

"After the New Year. It isn't a good idea to bring a puppy into the chaos that is Christmas," Hector decided.

"After New Year, then. We'll keep quiet about it and tell them it's a late Christmas present and that Santa didn't want the puppy to get spooked by the packages and wrapping paper and the tree. They have to walk it and feed it, though. It will be their dog," Steele agreed.

Steele and Hector quickly cleaned the kitchen and then called the boys. Hector raised his voice. "We're ready to go!"

"We're coming." Matteo ran into the kitchen, holding Felipe's hand.

"Uh...Papa, can I ask where we're going?" Matteo asked gingerly.

"We're going out to get decorations for the tree and lights," Hector answered.

"Do we get to pick some?" Felipe pulled on Steele's belt.

Matteo hissed, "Felipe...it's enough we're getting a tree."

Steele knelt in front of Matteo. "In this house, you will never get in trouble for asking. If we don't think that what you want is appropriate, we'll say no, just like that sugared cereal you wanted me to get. But don't be afraid. You'll never get in trouble for asking."

Matteo nodded and said in a small voice, "Can we pick some out?"

"We're going to the Christmas shop in Old Town, and each of us is going to pick one special ornament so we can remember our first Christmas together."

"Did you hear that, Matteo? We can pick. Here, we're allowed to pick. You told me it's going to be good; now you have to believe it, too." Felipe grabbed his brother and gave him a big hug.

Chapter Eleven

Tuesday Evening

Hector and Steele were getting ready for bed. Steele gave him a heated stare as Hector was changing his boxers for sleep pants. "You want to take a shower together?" Steele purred.

"What about the boys?" Hector seemed uncertain, but his cock rose.

"That's the beauty of them being upstairs." Steele grabbed his hand and pulled him into the shower, turning the water on.

"Are you sure you want to do this in the shower?" He moved his hand down Steele's chest.

Steele stared at Hector's lips. "I'll take you any way I can get you."

Steele captured him between his arms and pushed him against the tile wall. With one hand on either side of the younger man's face, his lips seized Hector's and took them in a hard kiss. Steele's mouth left Hector's lips and traced his jawline licking at the water rivulets that fell from his face.

He dropped to his knees. Hector's shaft was like

polished granite, smooth and hard. He took Hector's cock down his throat, massaging it with his throat muscles. He moved his lips up and down, sucking and licking to the sound of Hector's moans.

Hector brought his hand up to Steele's head and ran his fingers through the brush cut as Steele worked his tongue around the head. He always marveled at Hector's perfect cock. It was eight inches with a nice circumference. It curved ever so slightly to the left and felt perfect in Steele's hand, mouth, and, if he was honest, in his ass.

"I'm close...." Hector whispered.

"I want inside you."

"Do you have a condom?"

"No, but I have two clean tests, one from just last week and one from when I first arrived here from LA. When I moved into your room, I saw yours on the dresser. I haven't been with anyone else since I first came to Albuquerque."

"I haven't been with anyone else since a year before I met you."

Steele laughed. "A bit of a dry spell?"

"I'll have you know, I'm picky," Hector rumbled.

"And I'm lucky that you picked me. I'll use the gel—"

"No, you won't be quick enough. I'll prepare myself." Hector pivoted his body so his chest hit the tile and shoved two fingers covered with the shower gel up his channel, stretching his sphincter. "Take me now."

"You didn't prepare yourself properly," Steele objected.

"Now, damn it, or I'll come on the tile and you won't get off."

Steele took his cock in hand and lined it up with

Hector's hole. He pushed past the first muscle. Hector panted.

"Are you all right?" Steele asked worriedly.

"I'm fine, damn it. Move." Hector pushed back.

He began to move slowly until he was seated and his balls met Hector's ass.

"Move faster. I'm not an old lady. I want it hard and fast tonight." Hector moaned.

Steele pistoned his cock in and out of his hole until Hector moaned continuously. "You hit my spot every time."

Steele smirked. "Just talented, I guess."

"I should pinch you for that arrogance. But my cock is in your hand and I want to come now." Hector pushed back—hard. His channel clenched as he came over Steele's fingers.

Steele managed two more strokes before he, too, succumbed.

Thanksgiving Morning

The boys woke up at eight. Steele and Hector were already at the computer, ordering gifts. Steele shut the laptop when he heard them on the stairs.

"Good morning. We're having a light breakfast because we're eating at one. Hector's making scrambled eggs and bacon. If you're hungry at eleven, you can have a bowl of the Honey Nut Cheerios." Hector got the eggs and bacon out of the fridge.

"I think we'll pass on the Cheerios. I want to be able to eat the turkey. Do you think they'll have mashed potatoes and stuffing with gravy?" Matteo asked.

"I can guarantee it." Steele laughed.

"Plus, there will be lots of other food. We'd like you to try some of everything, so you can get used to a varied diet," Hector told them.

"We promise we'll try anything you put on our plate. We've eaten more different things this week than we ever have in our life, and everything has tasted good." Matteo smacked his lips. "I can't wait for turkey."

"If I know Debra, we'll probably have a ham, too," Steele promised. "If we don't, we'll make one for Christmas Eve."

"Will there be pie?" Felipe whispered. "I've never had pie."

"There will be pies. Apple, pumpkin, pecan, and custard pies plus a peach tart, from what Aden said." Hector put the bacon into a skillet then cracked eight eggs into a bowl and scrambled them with milk.

Ten minutes later, breakfast was ready. Felipe got out the placemats, and Matteo set the table and poured milk and juice for him and his brother. Steele poured the coffee, and Hector served up breakfast.

When they finished, Matteo helped clear. He picked up the heavy serving platter and winced. Hector took it from him. "Your arm hurts. I'll get the Tylenol for you. Then we can watch the parade on the big television and, after it's over, get ready to leave at noon."

"Where do Aden and Dr. Dare live?" Felipe asked.

"Placitas...." Steele was about to continue when Matteo whistled.

"I thought only rich people live there." Matteo said.

"People in Placitas may have a little more money, but they are mostly older and don't have kids. The school district isn't that good, so if you live in Placitas, you have to send your children to private school after fifth grade," Steele told Matteo.

"Will they care that I'm gay in the school here?" Matteo asked with trepidation.

"If you have problems in school because you're gay, we'll send you to one of the academies," Hector promised. "But they have a no tolerance for bullies policy in Rio Rancho, so we should be okay."

"We'll worry about that come Monday when the two of you start school. Hector and I bought you five outfits each for school until Christmas, when I'm sure Santa will be bringing you some nice clothing."

"When did you do that, Dad?" Felipe asked.

"When you were at the store buying your Thanksgiving clothes," Steele said.

"But I didn't see any other packages...." Matteo stated, curiosity painted all over his face.

"I took them out to the trunk of the Navigator. If you open your closet and drawers, you'll find new jeans, rugby shirts, long-sleeved graphic T-shirts, and a few sweaters, underwear, and socks."

Matteo's eyes shone with tears. "For both of us...?"

"For both of you. There may be times when you get something that Felipe doesn't or he gets something you don't, but we'll always be fair. There are no favorites in this house." Steele knelt by Matteo's chair, attempting to reassure him.

Matteo threw his arms around Steele's neck and hugged him tightly. Steele could feel the dampness of his tears on the shoulder of his shirt. "Easy, son. It's going to be all right. If it isn't, tell Papa or me, and we'll try to fix it. Now let's watch the parade.

Dare and Aden's Home
Thanksgiving Day Afternoon

The boys were stuffed after the big dinner. They had their turkey, dressing, and mashed potatoes, with candied yams, broccoli with hollandaise, creamed onions, green beans with almonds, and all kinds of pies and dessert. Each of the boys had to loosen the belt on their pants.

They boys played with Ranger, Monk, Trouble, and Bandit. Matteo and Felipe seemed taken with the dogs. "I'll guess we're getting one," Hector whispered to Steele.

Steele watched the boys play with the animals. "I guess so."

The adults sat down for coffee. "Those are wonderful boys. It's amazing, considering they practically raised themselves," Debra remarked. "Can they come over next Wednesday to make Christmas cookies? We'll be at it all day. I want to make enough for everyone. Aden is going to help. Dare will be the gofer. He's useless in the kitchen." Debra laughed.

"You malign me," Dare protested. "I learned how to make good coffee. You're drinking my coffee, and I clean and do the wash."

"There is that," Aden giggled as he and Dare started to clean the table. Dare saw Matteo and Felipe take notice.

"If you tell us where to put the plates, we can help," Matteo offered. Felipe stood up behind him.

"You're helping by keeping the dogs busy. Do you like dogs?"

"Oh, yes. Ranger and Monk are big, though." Felipe giggled and covered his eyes as Monk jumped over him to play some more.

"You might like a smaller dog." Dare got down on the floor and rolled around with the dogs who were all over him.

"If you watch Felipe with the dogs, I'll help Aden clear." Matteo got off the floor.

Dare turned his eyes toward Steele and Hector who shook his head. Dare put his arm around Matteo. "You have one job here today and that is to have fun. I have some video games in the great room. How about I set you and Felipe up to play. Aden has baseball games and football games. Do you like sports?"

"Yes, but I couldn't play. I had chores, and I had to take care of Felipe," Matteo answered without an ounce of self-pity.

"Now you have your Dad and Papa to take care of Felipe, and if they aren't around, you have Uncle Dare, Uncle Aden, and Grandma Schaeffer."

"Don't forget Uncle Jerry." Sanchez laughed.

"See, you have loads of people to take care of Felipe while you play a sport. Which sport do you like?"

"Baseball. When my father and mother weren't around, Felipe and I played catch. The neighbors gave us a tennis ball."

Dare watched the storm clouds appear over Steele and Hector's faces. "Well, now, outside of when you're at school or doing homework, you can play catch anytime you want except when you're sleeping," Dare teased.

Matteo giggled.

"It's not too cold outside. You and Felipe can take turns throwing the Frisbee to Ranger and Monk." Dare fetched their coats and the Frisbee, and showed Matteo and Felipe how to throw so the dogs could catch.

Once the boys were settled outside, Dare came in for coffee and a second piece of pie.

"I'm a doctor and even I believe that their parents should be shot." Dare shook his head in disgust.

"I know. The more we find out, the more outraged we become. We have to get them to surrender the kids for adoption. There has to be a way," Hector said.

"Maybe a little reverse psychology might work. Tell the mother how hard it would be for the boys. Tell her that they would be separated. If she hates them enough, and from what I've seen and heard, she does, she might release them if she thought they'd suffer. The dad would definitely release them if he thought it would cause them harm. Especially after Matteo told the DEA where to find the drugs and the guns. She can't be too happy, either. She's on the hook along with him for everything they did, including abusing the boys," Sanchez offered.

"We should ask Beatrice. It could backfire if she still wants her younger son just to be difficult," Dare observed.

"I think we ought to give the system a chance. If it seems like things aren't going our way, then we can play mind games with her. He doesn't need any mind games. I think both kids were accidental pregnancies, and he'd like to get rid of both of them." Steele took another slice of the pumpkin pie with hard sauce.

"I agree with Steele," Sanchez said. "You should have seen him cursing out his sons. He wants to do bodily harm to both of them. Now Beatrice has to get a judge to see it our way and terminate their rights."

***

Hector was in the kitchen, getting himself another slice of pecan pie, when Steele walked up behind him. "You know, it seems as if Jerry Sanchez has fully integrated himself into our little group. We'll see what happens with Rivers," Steele mused.

"It appears Sanchez is eager. I wonder about Rivers." Hector cut another slice of pie for Steele and then went to the window to watch the boys play with the dogs.

By six, the boys had exhausted themselves. After eating a second meal—Debra brought ham in pineapple sauce—they were both yawning.

"I think it's time for us to leave you guys to the football games. I've got two sleepyheads here." Hector ruffled both boys' hair.

"Go give everyone a kiss and a hug good-bye," Steele instructed.

When Matteo stopped by Debra's chair, he whispered, "Are you really going to be our grandmother?"

Debra gave them a hug. "Definitely. You live a few blocks away from me, so when I'm home, you can come over for milk and cookies."

Aden piped up, "My mom makes the best cookies. But you're going to find that out next week. Uncle Dare and I are picking you up early on Wednesday to take you to Grandma's so you can help her make Christmas cookies. Wednesday is our day off."

"Can we make some for Santa?" Felipe asked, excitement in his eyes.

"Of course," Debra answered.

"Maybe, if we have cookies, he won't forget where we live," Felipe said wistfully.

"He definitely won't forget where you live." Jerry pulled out his wallet. "You see these green cards?"

Matteo took his glasses out. "Now that I have my glasses, I can see everything," he said proudly.

"Me, too." Felipe showed everyone his glasses.

"If you examine them, you'll see they are copies of the change of address cards we sent to Santa for the two of you. It has the FBI seal on it so Santa will know it's official. A card like this gets top priority in his workshop." Jerry gave them each a card.

Matteo's mouth hung open. He knew there was no Santa but was so happy that they did this for his brother he almost started to cry.

Felipe jumped up and down. "He won't forget us this year, and we'll have cookies for him, too!"

Matteo hugged his brother. "What do you say to Grandma and Uncle Jerry?"

Felipe blushed. "Thank you. It will be the first Christmas that he knows where we are."

Everyone at the table eyes got sort of misty.

Aden got up. "Does anyone want more of Dare's coffee?"

"I'll take some," Jerry said.

"We'll get ours and the boys' coats off the bed and get going. I have a lot of point and click to do tomorrow and a few places either Hector or I have to go in person."

"You're not braving the stores on Black Friday?" Debra laughed.

"Well, I'm not going at midnight if that's what you mean. I'm not searching for any deals, but there are a few things we need that can't come from the

Internet in case they have to be exchanged. So, I'm going out tomorrow and Hector will go on Saturday." Steele put his hands on the boys' shoulders. "Get a move on, you two."

Felipe ran for the coats, but Matteo stayed behind and stared up at Steele. "He really is going to have a Christmas this year." Although it was a statement, there was still a question mark in his voice.

Steele messed with his hair, "Don't worry, you both are."

"You don't have to for me...."

"Are you my son?" Steele asked.

Unsure of the correct answer, Matteo whispered, "Yes."

"Well, everyone in the house gets Christmas, including Hector and me."

"Wow...." Matteo murmured.

"Wow indeed," Steele countered.

Hector, Steele, and the boys put on their coat and got into the car to go home.

Chapter Twelve

Thanksgiving Evening, Dare and Aden's House

"Those two boys have to be able to stay with Hector and Steele. The night I met Matteo, I thought he didn't even know how to smile. This afternoon, he was all about shy smiles and taking care of his brother." Aden started to take away the dessert dishes and wrap the pies.

"I'm glad we gave a few pies to Hector to take home and freeze. Their meal repertoire has expanded nicely, and they can make good comfort food, but pie crust is still beyond them, even when they buy the pre-packaged crust." Dare scraped the plates and put them in the dishwasher.

"Steele has brownie and muffin mix down pat. He even brings some into work occasionally, but the rest seem to be beyond his capacity." Sanchez chuckled.

"Nonsense," Debra interjected. "When I go to babysit, I'll teach Matteo how to make pound cake from a box. Then we'll progress to layer cake with canned frosting. That's how I taught Aden to cook."

"Mom, here, with cake, you have the altitude

problem."

"Pish tush, there are directions on the box for that," Debra said.

"I assume you plan on volunteering to do a lot of babysitting." Aden regarded her strangely.

"I've meant to talk to you. You know I told you I have more than enough so that I don't have to work anymore."

Aden dropped his jaw.

"Close your mouth, pumpkin. You're starting to resemble a fish."

Dare cracked up in the background. Sanchez hid his laugh behind a cough.

"Well, I sold a novel to a publisher. So far, it going to be an e-book, but I have high hopes. I sold it, and it's the first one I've ever written." The pride was evident in Debra's voice.

"What kind of novel, Mom?" Aden was curious. His mom had never been into fiction.

"It's a romance, and it will be published in March. Janet at the office turned me on to romances," I'm quitting work and becoming a writer. It's what I always wanted to do, and now I have enough investment income to live very well off the proceeds and do what I always wanted to do, which is write."

"Congratulations, Mom, but what's that got to do with babysitting?" Aden cocked his head waiting for the explanation.

"Well, Hector does shift work, although Steele's hours are steady. When Hector and Steele aren't home, somebody has to watch those boys. I remember you at ten; you were a pistol. Matteo is much better behaved than you were."

Aden said, "Mommmmm."

Dare came up and kissed his neck. "So you weren't always a good little pumpkin."

"Anyway, you can't leave kids that age alone, and poor Matteo has spent enough time taking care of his brother. I can write anytime and be available when they need me. After all," Debra said pointedly, "it will be a while before you two provide me with grandchildren to spoil. And if there were ever boys in need of spoiling by a doting grandma, it's those two."

"Have you talked about this with Hector or Steele?" Dare asked, knowing she hadn't.

"I wanted to meet the boys first. Their upbringing could have made them incorrigible, in which case I couldn't handle them. But they are very well behaved. I could say too well behaved. I'd like to see both of them get into some mild mischief. We'll see how it goes with the cookies. It can only help their cause with the state if there is a grandmother nearby to take up the slack if Hector and Steele pick up a case that takes a lot of their time."

Sanchez nodded. "That's true. Remember how much time Bruno Wysocki took? And that started out simply. Steele and Hector were busy almost twenty-four/seven for a good six weeks at the end."

"The state is sure to ask what arrangements they have in place to take care of the boys if one of them is stuck on a big case. Although Steele is head of the division and doesn't do much fieldwork anymore."

"Well, Mom, the people you need to talk to about this just left." Aden started the dishwasher and put out some more coffee and aperitifs.

Debra had a smug expression on her face. "I got their phone number from Hector to make arrangements for the kids to help with the cookies. The boys are all excited, and it will give the adults the opportunity to shop and wrap gifts. Steele said something about bicycles. I'll have to remind them to get helmets."

Jerry got up from the table. "I want to thank you for including me. It was an absolutely wonderful dinner. Aden did you proud, Debra. Jon Rivers is coming for Christmas at Hector and Steele's. He's the head of the DEA in Albuquerque."

"They're going to try and fix you up. Are you okay with that, Jerry?" Dare sipped his Irish Cream.

"Hell, yes. Rivers is handsome, understands the pressures of the job, and doesn't do undercover. If we click, he's perfect for me. I've already overstayed my welcome, so I'll get my coat and say good night." Jerry went into the bedroom, retrieved his coat, shook Dare and Aden's hand, and gave Debra a kiss then left the house.

"Since everything is cleaned up...." Debra turned to Dare with a mischievous sparkle in her eyes. "You do good work, Dare; it's my turn to leave."

Debra kissed both of them. Dare got her coat, and Aden walked her to her car.

"Good night, Mom."

"Good night, pumpkin. I'll call you later in the week. We have to do something spectacular for those boys for Christmas. Santa forgot where they lived, indeed." Debra went off in high dudgeon. "When I think about what those poor boys have suffered, I want to chop their parents' arms off and beat them with the bloody end."

Aden laughed. He knew his Mom. Debra was going to do everything in her power to make sure the boys stayed exactly where they were, even if that meant bearding Beatrice Marks in her den.

Thanksgiving Evening at Hector and Steele's

"It's only seven. You boys can watch TV with us, if you like. I'll make some popcorn." Hector took out a bag of Orville Redenbacher from the cabinet.

"Go on up and get into your pajamas, robes, and slippers. I'll turn on the TV and start a fire while Hector pops the popcorn. Is football all right with everyone?" Steele retrieved some wood from the patio.

"Uh...Dad, could you explain the rules to Felipe and me?" Matteo asked. "We weren't allowed to watch much TV, and I'd like to understand. All of the boys talk about the games at school, and I feel dumb because I don't know what they're talking about."

"Sure. The first thing you have to know is that our team is the Denver Broncos, not Texas or Arizona. Denver, got it?"

Matteo nodded.

"Broncos, like the horses?" Felipe chimed in.

"Yes, like the horses." Steele put together the fire, topped it with kindling, and lit the match. The smoke curled upwards, and soon there was a cheery fire in the great room. "Now, go up, change, hang up your clothes, and wash your hands. When you come down, Papa and I will explain the rest."

Hector regarded Steele with some amusement. "What if I was a Cowboys fan?"

Steele came from behind him, putting his arms around Hector's taut waist, and laved his earlobe. "Then I'd have to seduce you away from the dark side."

"Speaking of the dark side, I bet the kids have never seen a single *Star Wars* movie. I have all of them on disk. We'll have to schedule a *Star Wars* marathon for some time before Christmas. If they like the movies, we can get them some of the toys. There is a new movie coming out; we can take them to see that one a couple of days after Christmas."

"Sounds like a plan. Are you a Cowboys fan?" Steele cringed.

"No, and unless New Mexico gets a pro team, I'm for Denver. We should take the kids to a Lobos game next season. UNM has a nice stadium." Hector's face lit up at the idea of taking the boys to see a live football game.

"This summer, we could take them to see the Isotopes play. They're the triple-A farm team for the Rockies. Matteo mentioned today that he'd like to play baseball. Football may be your game, but baseball was mine." Hector took the popcorn out of the microwave and melted some extra butter.

"I've never played soccer. What if they like soccer?" Steele asked.

"One of the others probably played soccer. Aden doesn't have the build for football or baseball, but I could definitely see him playing soccer as a kid." Hector thought about it. "We can consult Dare, Jerry, and Jon for help if we need it. I'm sure all of them played one sport or another. Here come the boys."

"Hey, guys, let's sit down and watch the Broncos," Hector said as he took Felipe and put him on his lap. Steele pulled Matteo under his arm, and the four of them watched the game with Steele patiently explaining the rules while they munched on buttered popcorn.

Black Friday Morning

Hector and Steele were up earlier than the boys. Steele was going to Corrales to the bike shops, and

Hector planned on beginning the *Star Wars* Marathon as soon as they finished breakfast.

Matteo came down the stairs dressed in jeans and a flannel shirt. "Did we miss breakfast? We had to take a shower because we didn't take one last night."

"Dad and I had breakfast early. We wanted you guys to sleep in. Both of you have dark circles under your eyes. You up for pancakes and bacon?"

"If you already had breakfast with Dad, Felipe and I could eat cereal, or I could make him eggs," Matteo offered.

"Did you take out the garbage yesterday?"

"Yes, Papa. You saw me do it."

"Is it time to take out the garbage yet today."

"No, you said to take it out at night, but if you want me to—"

"What I want is for you to get ready for a *Star Wars* marathon after I fix you pancakes and bacon. You did your chore yesterday, and, later on tonight, you'll do it again, so don't ask me about making breakfast unless there is an emergency. I'm here; I'll make breakfast. Are we good?" Hector took the milk out of the refrigerator and pulled the pancake mix off the shelf.

"Yes, Papa, we're good. I'll tell Felipe we have pancakes and bacon. Pancakes are his favorite." Matteo turned to get his brother.

Hector stopped him by putting his hand on Matteo's shoulder. "What's your favorite breakfast?"

"Oatmeal with maple and brown sugar," Matteo answered right away.

"You didn't even have to think about it." Hector was astonished. Matteo had expressed a preference. One he didn't even have to think about.

"I had a babysitter once, and she made it for supper at her house. I really liked it. It came in little packets. All you have to do is put in hot water. Can we have that?" Matteo put his hand over his mouth as if he were shocked he'd actually asked.

"I can do better than that. I'll use real cooked oatmeal, not the stuff in packets, and we can add our own maple syrup and brown sugar. We'll see how you like that." Hector smiled at his new son.

"Really, Papa? You can make it without the packets?" Matteo grinned.

"Yes, you can. I'll call Dad and have him bring some brown sugar and regular oatmeal home. We have real maple syrup. So we can have it tomorrow for breakfast along with some toast and ham. Go get your brother for breakfast, and I'll call Dad."

Hector picked up his cell phone from the counter and pushed the speed dial for Steele.

"Adams...."

"You should read at your caller ID once in a while. If I were one of the kids, you would have scared the pants off him."

"I'm in a sea of bicycles. We've decided on a BMX for both boys with a twenty-inch wheelbase for Matteo and a sixteen-inch base for Felipe. Now I have to decide what brand and what bells and whistles. What do you need, my love?"

"I like that 'my love.' You can keep that one in your flirting repertoire. I need you to bring home oatmeal that you cook. Quaker Oats. Read the directions and make sure it's not the one that you prepare by just dumping in boiling water. Our son has finally asked for something. Oatmeal with maple and brown sugar. I need light brown sugar, too." Hector mixed the pancake batter and oiled the griddle with a mixture of butter and vegetable oil.

"Matteo actually asked for something for himself?" Steele sounded astounded.

"I backed him into a corner, but he asked, and he's getting it tomorrow morning even if I have to import Aden to make it. Also, bring home a quart of half and half. My abuela used to serve her oatmeal with cream." In a separate pan, Hector turned the bacon.

"Done, done, and done. Matteo will have oatmeal tomorrow. We're finally making progress. The therapist will be glad to hear it. I hear cooking sounds. Get back to breakfast while I further immerse myself in bicycle lore. After this, I'm going to J.C. Penny to buy the boys some Christmas clothing. Are we dressing for Christmas?"

"Lord, no." Hector lowered his voice. "The boys are going to want to play with their toys; they can't do that dressed up. Maybe next year we'll take them to a church that accepts us and they can dress for church. But this year is all about fun." Hector flipped the pancakes

"We need to take Felipe to see Santa at the mall," Steele said.

"We're going to have to wait in line for an hour. We'll get them up early tomorrow so we'll be first in line."

"It's a deal. Now go plate breakfast. Our boys are hungry. I love you, baby."

"I love you, too, *mi corazón*." Hector put down the phone. "Boys, breakfast is ready. After that, you're going to watch the *Star Wars* movies with me. Do you want to see them in the order they were made, or in the correct timeline?"

"What's a timeline?" Felipe wanted to know.

"Monday, Tuesday, Wednesday is a timeline, the days of the week in a row. George Lucas, the creator of Star Wars, made the three for Tuesday first. Then he made the three for Monday and coming up at Christmas is the first of the three for Wednesday. What do you think? Tuesday's are better than Monday's. Wednesday we aren't sure of yet."

"Felipe, what do you think?"

"You decide, Matteo."

"I think seeing the second three will spoil the first three because you know what's going to happen. Let's watch the first three. We know the second three are better and have something to look forward to," Matteo said after seeming to give the matter some thought.

"Then that's what we'll do. Come on, the pancakes are getting cold."

Chapter Thirteen

Black Friday, J.C. Penney

Steele's phone vibrated in his pocket. It was a text from Hector. *U coming home. W8 lunch 4 u?*

Steele texted back. *J.C. Penny a zoo. 1 hour, maybe more. Feed boys. I eat here.*

OK, don't go nuts. I do rest 2morrow. Best Buy by Penny's. Need to check gaming sys & phones. Hector replied.

Luv u. Steele sent.

Luv u 2.

Steele grinned.

***

Steele called Dare and went to stow the two bikes in his garage.

"Do you want some coffee and leftover pie?" Aden asked.

"No, thanks. I want to go home and have a beer. The boys and Hector are watching movies and, after being immersed in bicycle gears all morning, and at the zoo that is the mall, buying the boys clothes, all I want to do is go home and put my feet up."

"The joys of fatherhood," Dare teased.

"Actually, despite my complaining, I had a good time. My only wish is that Hector and I could have done it together."

"Next time, call one of us or my mother. We'll either go over and watch the boys for a few hours or they can come over here or go to her house. Then you can go with Hector," Aden offered.

"I may take you up on that. I'm a bit overwhelmed. They've never had anything, and I know we can't buy them everything at once even though I want to buy out the store. I bought bicycles today. A phone will be necessary for Matteo's peace of mind, and a gaming system that the whole family can play is a good idea. I want to buy both boys baseball gear and a football. Neither one of us knows anything about soccer." Steele parked the bikes in the third bay of the garage.

"I played basketball, and Aden did gymnastics. Ask Rivers or Sanchez about soccer. Rio Rancho has a community pool. They should also know how to swim."

"Hold it, Dare. I can't make up for ten years of depredation in one week. I'll get them swimming lessons come spring, and Hector and I will teach them sports if they want to learn, but they need some time to acclimate to their new life, to settle into the house and our lives." Steele walked out to his Navigator.

"You're right. I'm not ready to be a father yet because I'd go and buy out the store and have them signed up for every lesson available." Aden examined the bikes. "Did you get them helmets? Mom wanted to remind you."

"Yes, I got helmets for both the bikes and baseball."

"You're good to go, then. We'll see you on Wednesday to pick up the boys to make cookies."

Black Friday Late Afternoon

Steele walked in the door as the last credits of the last of the first three movies rolled by on the television. "Was it good watching on the sixty-five-inch television?"

Felipe ran to Steele before he could get his coat off. "Dad, we watched three movies, three! Papa said the next three are even better, and, after that, we can go to the movies to see the new one!" Felipe was like a jumping bean he was so excited.

"Whoa there, chipmunk. I gather you saw the first three *Star Wars* movies. What did you think, Matteo?"

"They were good. I loved the lightsabers and Yoda. I can't believe Anakin Skywalker turned to the Dark Side and that Obi-Wan blamed himself."

Steele lifted his eyes over Matteo's head to Hector."

"Hello, *mi corazón*, I guess you have the answer to your question. I'm glad you brought the TV out of storage. The boys really enjoyed seeing the movie on the larger screen." Hector gave Steele a light kiss. "Did you have a productive day?"

"Yes, I dropped the two large packages off at Dare's. The rest we'll bring in tonight. I'm all for pointing and clicking for the rest of it and doing our research online. I know, for certain items, you have to go to Best Buy, but I suggest you go late at night or early in the morning. There were too many people. I had one woman elbow me with her purse then grab a sweater out of my hand." Steele shook his head.

"Go sit down and I'll get you a beer. I'm sure there is football on somewhere." Hector chuckled. "I made beef stew for dinner with some Bisquick biscuits."

"Aden's recipe?"

"Of course, although I did see an interesting recipe in the cookbook he gave us when you moved into the house. It's called Belgian Beef and Beer Stew." Hector raised an eyebrow.

"I like our stew just the way it is. Do you need any help in the kitchen?"

"No, just sit down and put your feet up. You've been on them all day. Let me get two beers and I'll join you on the couch."

"Thank you, baby. I'm tired. Do I get kisses and hugs from my boys after coming home from the store wars?"

Felipe threw himself into Steele's arms. "I missed you, Dad. Papa, Matteo, and I want to watch the rest of the movies with you."

Matteo followed Felipe and gave Steele a quick kiss and hug. "You'll watch the rest of them with us?"

"Sure, I let poor Papa watch the ones that weren't so good with you. We'll watch the first good one together. I'll even make the popcorn with extra butter." Steele laughed.

"I think I'm going to let you go to the Sports Authority tomorrow while I go shopping with the boys. That will show you not to bait the bear in his den." Hector growled and came after Steele. The boys started to giggle.

Early Evening

"We'll all go to the mall together to see the boys with Santa at eight thirty. Then I'll go to the Sports Authority, and you can go with the boys to Best Buy. I'll put the mitts, bats, baseball, and football in the car and come to Best Buy and get the boys. After you finish there, we can meet up at Toys R Us where we can find out what they like and then buy it online. How does that sound?" Steele suggested.

"It sounds like a plan." Hector turned to him. "Do you want a beer?"

"No, I've got a bit of indigestion. I'll take a Coke if you're going that way." Steel put his hand to his chest.

"Are you okay? You appear pale," Hector said worriedly.

Sweat began to form on Steele's brow. "I don't feel very well. My chest hurts."

"I'm calling an ambulance." Hector ran for the phone.

"I'm all right. I have indigestion."

***

As soon as Hector got off the phone, he ran to the medicine cabinet and got Steele an aspirin. "Take the aspirin."

Steele took the pill out of Hector's hand. "You're overreacting." Steele swallowed the pill with a sip of water.

"No, I'm not. We have two boys to raise *together*, and I love you and refuse to lose you so soon. I'm calling Debra to watch the kids."

Debra pulled up at the same time the ambulance arrived. She ran into the house, seeing Hector wringing his hands. "Go, follow Steele. I called Dare and Aden on my way here. They'll be waiting at the hospital."

"I have to talk to the boys first. I don't want them to be frightened." Hector went upstairs. He found Felipe and Matteo huddled in Matteo's bed.

"Is Dad okay? Will we have to leave?" Matteo was panicking.

"Uncle Dare and Uncle Aden will take care of him. Grandma is downstairs. You do whatever she says. I'll be back with Dad soon, and, no, you don't have to leave."

Hector ran to the garage, hopped into the Explorer, and followed the ambulance the nine miles to the University of New Mexico Sandoval Medical Center, praying that he hadn't lied to the boys.

He pulled in the parking lot of the emergency room, grabbed his keys, and pushed the button to lock his vehicle while he ran into the ambulance bay.

He stopped an EMT he knew who had taken Steele out of the house. "What's going on? That's my partner."

"You'll have to talk to Rourke, but I think he had a mild heart attack. Go inside and check in at the desk so they know you're here.

The ER admin asked for Steele's information. "I'm glad I remembered to bring his wallet," Hector told her sarcastically."

"Sheriff Gomez, I have to do my job, just as you have to do yours. I need this information for Mr. Adams' own protection," the medical receptionist said.

Hector examined her face. "I shouldn't take my fear and frustration out on you." Hector took Steele's wallet from his pocket. The admin photocopied Steele's insurance card and his license.

"I'll put this data in his chart. Do you know if he has any allergies or other medical conditions that the doctor should know about?" She was reading from the screen and typing in Steele's insurance number and his driver's license number.

"The wallet is all I have to go on. We just got engaged yesterday. I don't know any his medical history yet."

"That's all right; tell me what you know. Mr. Adams will be able to speak for himself in about two hours. Dr. Rourke is taking good care of him."

Hector sat down wearily in the waiting room. The door opened, and Hector saw Debra with the kids, his deputies, Sanchez and Rivers. Both boys ran into his arms with Debra right behind them. "I'm sorry, Hector. The boys were hysterical."

"Papa, what happened to Dad?" Felipe asked, fear evident on his face.

"I don't know yet, but I think he had a mild heart attack."

"Is he going to die?" Matteo asked, tears pouring down his cheeks.

"Dr. Dare and Aden are taking care of him right now." Hector's eyes slid to Debra.

"They had to be here. Jerry called about something work-related, and, well, here we all are. He convinced me that it was better for the boys to be here rather than at home not knowing what was happening. I think he's right. They're still crying, but they seem calmer."

"Garcia? Why is the whole shift here instead of

on patrol?"

"Jesus, Gomez. Adams is a friend. When we heard the call, we came right away. We were worried about Adams and the boys."

"Dare and Aden are taking care of Steele. I'll keep you updated, but you guys have to go back out on patrol. Someone has to be available to take radio calls. What would have happened to Steele if all of you were here?"

Edwards and White shuffled their feet. "Yes, boss."

Garcia patted Hector on the back. "I'm not on duty. I'll stay with you and the boys. Let me get them something to eat. It will give them something to do."

At that moment, Dare came through the door. "He's resting. He had two occluded arteries. There is very little damage to the heart. I have an information sheet as to what he needs to do when he goes home. Don't let him talk you into doing more."

Hector read the pamphlet.

Home Care After a Heart Attack
Take it easy for the first 4 - 6 weeks.
Avoid heavy lifting.
Get some help with household chores if you can.
Take 30 - 60 minutes to rest in the afternoon for first 4 - 6 weeks. Try to go to bed early and get plenty of sleep.
Before starting to exercise, your doctor will do an exercise test and recommend an exercise plan. This may happen before you leave the hospital or soon afterward. Do not change your exercise plan before talking with your health care provider.
You should be able to talk comfortably when you are doing any activity—such as walking, setting

the table, and doing laundry. If you cannot, stop the activity.

Ask your doctor about when you can return to work. Expect to be away from work for at least 4 - 6 weeks.

Wait at least 2 weeks before sexual activity. Ask your doctor when it is okay to start again. Do not take Viagra, Levitra, Cialis, or any herbal remedy for erection problems without checking with your doctor first.

"Papa, does that mean no kisses or hugs?" Matteo asked, very concerned.

"No, that item doesn't apply to you. It's for Steele and me."

"Okay." Hector thanked God that Matteo let it go. The ER was no place for the sex lecture, but with Matteo's early puberty, that would come soon enough. Hector watched Matteo read the rest of it.

How long you will have to wait to return to your normal activities will depend on:

Your physical condition before your heart attack

The size of your heart attack

If you had complications

The overall speed of your recovery

Diet and Lifestyle

Do not drink any alcohol for at least 2 weeks. Ask your doctor when you may start. Limit how much you drink. Men should have no more than 2 alcoholic drinks a day. Try to drink alcohol only when you are eating.

Hector finished reading. "I have questions....

How bad was the attack?"

"It was a mild heart attack, but it was a warning. He needs to eat a healthier diet, which will be good for the boys and you, too. Also, he needs to get some exercise, join a gym. I'm signing him up for cardio physical therapy starting the Monday after next." Dare adjusted his lab coat over his scrubs.

"He works out...." Hector protested.

"I'll bet he does more strength training than cardio. He has to do cardio. We'll do a stress test sometime next week."

"That's where you have him on the treadmill?"

"Yeah. He's going to be fine as long as he follows my instructions." Dare glanced at the electronic chart in his hand.

"He's going to be difficult," Hector warned.

Dare eyes met his. "I trust you and the boys to ride herd on him. I'll make an appointment with a nutritionist after the holidays. In the meantime, use common sense. Research a heart healthy diet on the web. Limit his red meat. Limit his fried food. Don't let him make butter and salt into their own food group."

"I don't think diet will be the problem. Making him rest, especially with Christmas coming...." Hector's gaze traveled across the room to the boys.

"Tell him if he wants to see next Christmas, he'll do the right thing. Make sure he rests and takes a short nap every day. The prescriptions I'm writing are going to make him a bit drowsy until his body adjusts. You saved his life by giving him that aspirin. That is why it was only a mild attack." Dare put his arm around Hector's shoulder.

"Basically, keep him quiet for two weeks. Aden and I will come over and help make Christmas for the boys. What you can't get online, tell us, and we'll pick it up. Debra will help you with the meal. The boys won't miss Christmas because of this, and that way Steele won't obsess over what isn't getting done."

"I don't know what to say." He gave Aden and Dare a hug. "Both of you are so good to us, it's an honor to be your friends."

"I'm going back to the recovery room to check on him. You should be able to see him in about ten minutes. You can bring the boys. I know they're anxious." Aden went back through the double doors leading to the surgical suite. Dare followed.

Chapter Fourteen

Black Friday, Later in the Evening

As soon as Dare and Aden left the room, Matteo was pulling at Hector's belt to get his attention. "If we made too much work for Dad and caused this, we can ask Ms. Marks to let us leave and go somewhere else." Tears were pouring out of his eyes.

"Let's get one thing straight, you didn't cause this. According to Uncle Dare, this would have happened no matter what we did because Dad wasn't taking care of himself long before you and Felipe came along." Hector knelt and opened his arms to both boys who ran into them. "You are our sons, and nothing is going to change that," he promised.

Felipe hugged him hard. "We don't have to leave?"

"No, you don't have to go. If someone says you have to leave, all four of us will move somewhere else. You don't have to leave us until it's time for you to go to college, and, even then, our house is still your home."

"You promise—"

Matteo interrupted. "Don't make him promise. Sometimes things happen that even adults can't do anything about."

"Matteo." Hector turned serious. "I promise."

Both boys started to cry again and held on tight.

"Now you have to wash your faces and hands and stop sniffling because we're going in to see Dad and we don't want to worry him. The bathroom is right over there."

Matteo took Felipe's hand and, armed with Hector's handkerchief, took Felipe to wash their faces and dry their eyes.

"I couldn't be prouder of those boys if they were my own flesh and blood," Debra Schaeffer announced to the room at large. She caught Hector's eye. "If Steele is coming home tomorrow, how about I take the boys for a sleepover tonight and you can get some more Christmas wrapping and other things done this evening. That way Steele will be relieved that it's being handled."

"Thank you, Debra. Steele wants the boys to have the best Christmas we can possibly make for them. Garcia, could you go over go the Sports Authority and buy the right size bat, mitts, and baseballs for the boys? We'll need a football and a soccer ball, too. Here." Hector handed Garcia three hundred dollars.

"I need someone to stay with Steele while I take the boys to have their picture taken with Santa Sunday morning." Hector glanced up and saw that Aden had come out of the recovery room.

"I'll do it, and I'll make sure he does no more than point and click while you're out," Aden volunteered, coming in at the tail end of the conversation.

"I need help with something else. We need a

gaming system for the house, handheld games for the boys, and telephones. Sanchez, do you know computers?"

"Yeah, I'm pretty good with electronics."

"If Debra is taking the boys tonight, Best Buy is open late. Maybe you could come with me to the Sports Authority and Best Buy. You can help me pick out that stuff. I'm not electronically inclined. That way Garcia gets to go home to his family."

Garcia handed the money back to Hector and guffawed. "I remember how badly you screwed up the patrol car computers when we first got them."

Sanchez cracked up. "Sure, I'll go with you. Rivers is good at that, too, and he plays sports."

Rivers joined them. "I'd be happy to play Uncle Jon and help."

"Yeah, I was counting on Steele to do the research to tell me what to buy. Speaking of computers, we need one for each of them. I don't know what to get." Hector grimaced, trying not to think about how Steele was feeling in the recovery room.

"We'll get them laptops with fourteen-inch screens where the keyboard lifts out of the way and the laptop becomes a tablet. They'll also need Kindles and iPods. Get them cheap phones until they are a bit older, smartphones, but without anything but basic functions, the net, texting, and a camera. You can trade up to better phones when you see how they take care of these," Sanchez told him.

Aden tapped his foot. "My patient is getting antsy because his partner and his kids aren't with him."

"Shit. I'll get the boys out of the men's room, and we'll go back." Hector pivoted and headed to the men's room.

***

Steele woke up to the *beep, beep* of monitors. He had an IV drip in his arm and felt a bandage by his groin. Aden was at the head of the bed.

"That'll teach you not to eat so much red meat and fried food," Aden chided.

"I gather I've had a heart attack. How bad?" Steele whispered, thinking of the physical he had to take to keep the boys.

"Very mild. Dare put in two stents. You'll be out of here by tomorrow morning. But Hector has a pamphlet of instructions you need to follow to completely recover." Aden noted his blood pressure, pulse, and respiration.

"I have to take a physical to keep the boys. Now I can't pass. I'll have to move out so they can stay with Hector." Steele clenched his fists.

"Whoa, John Wayne...before you ride off into the sunset, and shoot yourself in the foot, talk to Dare. You'll be up and able to do anything reasonable in six weeks, even return to work."

"I can?" Steele was amazed and relieved.

"Hector will have Beatrice let Dare give you the physical. He won't lie, but he said there was only slight damage to the heart. Hector gave you an aspirin just in time. You're perfectly capable of taking care of the boys. Now, the kids are scared and want to see you. I'm going to go get them and Hector." Aden left the room.

Steele peered around the room. He was the only one there. He picked up his wrist, no watch. They must have taken his watch off when he went to the

OR. Upon further examination, he found a clock on the wall. It read eight. He had sat on the couch with Hector at four.

Steele heard a commotion at the door. He lifted his head and smiled. Hector could barely hold the boys back from jumping on his bed.

"*Mi corazón*, you managed to scare us all." Hector leaned over and kissed him. He turned to Felipe and Matteo. "Here now, you see Dad is okay. He'll be home in the morning. Have Uncle Aden give you the pamphlet, Matteo, so you know what's going on. Now, say good night to Dad and go home with Grandma for a sleepover. She'll stop at our house to get your night things. Here are the keys. Tell her I'll let myself in from the garage."

Matteo took Felipe by the hand, climbed the bed railing, and kissed Steele. Hector lifted up Felipe so he could do the same. "Good night, Dad. I'm glad you're okay. We won't watch the other *Star Wars* movies without you."

"My chipmunk isn't chattering. Don't worry, Felipe. I'm going to be fine. Uncles Dare and Aden promised. And, just in case you're wondering, Santa is still coming." Steele chuckled.

Aden took the boys out to Debra.

"We both have to clean up our acts. This could just as easily have been me. I ate the same diet you did. The good news is you're going to be okay. The bad news is no sex for two weeks."

"Not even a little fooling around?" Steele laughed.

"Just cuddling for you. It will be all that much better when we can." Hector kissed him again. "Seriously, *mi corazón*, I almost lost you. If you hadn't taken the aspirin, I might have. We have boys now. We have to take care of ourselves. Besides, I love you and you're not allowed to leave me."

"I love you, too, baby. All I could think about in the ambulance on the way over was you and the boys. I thought I'd have to leave because of the physical necessary to be a foster parent, but Aden told me it would be okay. What are we going to do about Christmas?"

"Handled. Sanchez, Rivers, and I are going to Best Buy and the Sports Authority when we leave here. The rest is point and click. I'll leave that to you since you have to rest. Debra is going to help with Christmas dinner and Aden, Dare, Sanchez, and maybe Rivers will help me wrap gifts and get the tree."

"I wanted to do that with you on our first Christmas together." Steele almost pouted.

"After I get the lights up, you can help hang the ornaments, ribbons, and bows."

"Ribbons and bows?" Steele perked up.

"Yes, instead of a tinsel garland, I use Christmas ribbon. I get cloth ribbon at Michaels. It makes the tree appear more festive. You'll see when you get home. You need to tell me where in the storage locker you put your Christmas stuff," Hector said. "I want to go there Sunday after I get the boys' pictures taken with Santa. It will make them feel better if I get your stuff to put on the tree, too."

"Hector, can we make it right with Beatrice? If we can't, I'll move out so they don't have to leave."

"Dare said he has it handled. He hasn't lied to us yet. I believe him." Hector glanced at his watch. "You need to sleep. Aden is coming to move you into a room. I'll go with Sanchez to get the rest of the boy's Christmas stuff while there are still things on the shelves to get. I'll be back to take you home early tomorrow morning."

Hector bent and kissed Steele. Steele grabbed him around the neck. "You know I love you, right? The idea of never seeing you and the boys again scared the piss out of me. I want you to know how much I care about all of you. I'm not great with words, as I've said, but know this, I love you and those boys more than anything I've ever cared about in my life, and I'll do nothing to jeopardize that." A tear rolled down Steele's cheek. He quickly brushed it away.

Hector leaned over the bed and kissed Steele's eyelids. "I love you, too, and our boys love and need both of us, so do what they tell you to do tonight and do the same when you come home. We can't lose you."

Steele nodded. "I'm tired. I think I'm going to take a nap."

"You do that, and I'll go with Sanchez and Rivers. Good night, *mi corazón.*"

"Good night, baby."

***

When Hector got out to the waiting room, it had cleared out. Debra, true to her word, had taken the boys. Garcia had gone home to his family, but Sanchez and Rivers sat in the corner, waiting for him. They stood.

"Are you ready to brave the stores? Remember, it's still Black Friday." Sanchez chuckled.

"I'm ready. I just hope shopping doesn't give *me* a heart attack," Hector said, only half-joking.

Saturday just after Midnight

Rivers and Sanchez left after bringing in all the packages. Hector took out his small ladder and placed the bags on top of the plywood he put in the top of the garage. He'd bought two Microsoft Surface Pro 2 computers, two Kindle Fires, an Xbox with all the bells and whistles, and two Nintendo DSI XLs. Jerry and Jon insisted on buying the boys their smartphones so they got them each a Nokia Lumina 530—a Windows compatible phone that the salesman said was a good starter smartphone for kids. The phones played music, so that eliminated the need to buy a separate iPod, and Hector decided on some nice padded headphones he saw at Best Buy with the extra money he saved not having to buy two iPods.

At Sports Authority, they bought all the required gear for Little League for both boys plus a football, basketball, and a soccer ball. Rivers told him to buy a miniature basket and basketball online for Felipe and to put up a regulation hoop on the front of the garage for Matteo.

The rest of it would be delivered by mail from either Amazon or Walmart. He'd keep Steele busy online so he wouldn't overtax himself with the other chores. He exited the garage and took out a Coke and sat at the kitchen table. The house felt like a tomb. After living by himself for fifteen years, now, after only six months with Steele and two weeks with the boys, he missed the noise. He even missed Steele's snoring. Hector finished his Coke and went to bed.

Chapter Fifteen

Saturday Morning

Hector was up and had eaten breakfast by seven. He called the hospital and found out that Dare had come in on his day off to personally discharge Steele. He put his dishes in the dishwasher, straightened up the bedroom, got into his Explorer, and headed for UNM Sandoval to pick up his heart.

Steele raised his head as soon as Hector came into the room. "Hi, baby. We have to stop at Walgreens. Dare left me four prescriptions."

"What are you going to be taking?" Hector sat on the bed, handing Steele clean clothes.

"Low-dose aspirin, a beta-blocker, an ACE inhibitor, and a statin for my cholesterol. Dare said I'll be taking them the rest of my life." Steele sighed.

"I'd make you drink piss if it meant I could keep you around until we're both very old men," Hector said, half-serious.

"Baby, I'd do most anything for you, but drinking piss is definitely off the table." Steele yawned.

"You okay to go home? You seem to be beat."

Hector watched him carefully.

"I find that I'm exhausted today. I want to go to the drugstore then home to take a nap in my own bed."

"Debra's not bringing the kids home until eleven. So you have time for a long nap before the boys come back."

"As much as I want to see them, I don't want to worry them with my fatigue. Dare said it was normal for the first few days. He told me I have to toe the line as far as food, sleep, and exercise or he'll throw me in a cardiac rehab facility. He wanted me to go, but I wanted to come home to you."

Hector helped Steele out of the hospital gown and into his sweats. "I'll make you toe the line. You proposed. You're not getting out of it that easy." He put on Steele's coat. "Put your hat and gloves on before you go outside. It's cold out today. Last night, it was only ten degrees."

Steele signed his discharge papers and Hector went out to get the car. He pulled the car around to the front of the hospital where Steele was waiting with the orderly.

***

The boys came back with Debra at eleven and found Steele dressed in his sweats and slippers, waiting for them on the sofa.

"Don't jump on him, Felipe. The pamphlet said he's got to take it easy for the first few days and he can't lift over ten pounds. Grandma let me use her computer, and I did a search." Matteo held onto his brother.

"I won't break if you come over and give me hugs

and kisses." Steele opened his arms. He drew the boys in, hugging them hard.

"Is there anything we can do for you, Dad?" Matteo asked.

"As a matter of fact, there is. I was searching for two boys to watch the next three *Star Wars* movies with me. Know anyone I can ask?"

Felipe jumped up and down, "Me...me!"

Hector came out of the kitchen and greeted Debra. "You were a godsend last night. Thank you."

"Those two boys are a pleasure to care for. If I had ahold of their parents, I'd smack them upside the head with a two by four. I gave them baths last night, and they still have discolorations from the bruising."

Steele said dryly, "I know, and Matteo still has a gunshot wound on his arm."

"I checked it last night and changed the dressing, but he isn't favoring that arm, so it should be fine. When the boys and I came by to pick up their things for the sleepover, Felipe showed me where the prescription ointment was kept, and I made sure Matteo took the last of his antibiotics. I'd ask for a cup of coffee, but I'm in a hurry. I want to catch the sales. I'll let you know what I get." Debra waved good-bye and sailed out the front door.

Matteo and Felipe went to find the Blu-ray discs of the next three *Star Wars* movies. Steele turned to Hector, "Why do I have the feeling we've created a granmonster? She's going to buy out the stores. Aden and Dare better do their surrogate thing quickly, or we are going to have to move out to make room for the kids' stuff."

The boys came back, and Hector inserted the first movie of the original trilogy into the player. Felipe sat on Hector's lap, and Matteo laid his head on Steele's lap, and the movie began. Halfway through the second movie, Steele took a nap.

Sunday after Thanksgiving

Aden showed up early Sunday morning. Hector dressed the boys in their Thanksgiving clothes to go see Santa. Hector let Steele sleep in and told Aden to wake him at ten. "We should be home by then."

The visit to Santa was emotional. Hector took the man aside and explained the situation. He was very accommodating and apologized profusely to Felipe and Matteo for misplacing their address. Then he asked them what they wanted for Christmas.

Matteo answered for both boys. "Our dad got sick yesterday. We want him to get better."

The man was as moved as Hector. "Your dad will get better," Santa told them after getting a thumbs-up sign from Hector. "But I also want to know what's on your list."

Felipe answered and Matteo agreed, "We decided on lightsabers from *Star Wars*."

Hector was close by when Santa asked "Is that it?" with some surprise. Both boys nodded.

"Well, Santa may find a few things in his sack you might like besides the lightsabers. Now, smile and get your pictures taken so your dad knows you saw Santa."

Hector waited for the photos and purchased six wallet size and four five by sevens. He was ready to go home to his man.

***

Aden got Steele up at ten and made him a breakfast of pancakes with syrup. Steele grumbled about missing his bacon.

"Hector saved your bacon on Friday when he gave you that aspirin. Now it's up to you to stay alive long enough to enjoy him and the boys. Bacon does not further that goal." Aden dished up the pancakes.

At eleven, Steele heard the garage door open. "As much as I enjoy your company, Aden, I missed Hector and the boys." Aden laughed and kissed him on the cheek.

"Tell Hector I couldn't stay. I need to go shopping for Dare. Behave yourself."

Steele wasn't as tired today. He went over the list of things the boys would need for school the next morning and checked to see if they had every one of the items listed. Hector would have to make a trip to Walmart for a few things they forgot, but it was all good.

Hector and the boys came in from the garage. "Aden couldn't stay?" Hector asked.

"He said he needed to go shopping for Dare." Steele grinned.

"That's going to take him a while. There isn't much Dare wants that he doesn't have except more free time with Aden."

"Uncle Aden was here?" Matteo asked. "I like Uncle Aden, so does Felipe. We like all of our new uncles, and we love Grandma. Grandma said she checked and Wednesday is an in-service day for the teachers, so we won't have school. We can still make cookies."

"Yes, I told Santa we'd give him cookies and that Uncles Aden and Dare and Grandma would help us make them," Felipe said proudly. "Santa said he was sorry he missed us but he'd see us this year. We have school tomorrow." He sighed.

"Speaking of school"—Hector sat the boys down—"I'm driving both of you to school tomorrow to make sure you are registered and so I can meet your teachers."

"You want to meet my teacher?" Matteo asked.

"Of course. How else do I know who to call if you're having a problem with schoolwork?"

"*They* never went to the conferences, even when the teacher sent a note asking to see them." Matteo frowned. It was apparent he wasn't sure if he liked this new development.

"If you need help, Steele and I need to know." Hector was very proactive. His own mama and papi had always been at the school, volunteering, acting as chaperones on trips, and attending each and every school function, even after ten kids. Hector was bound and determined that his boys would have the same kind of attention.

"Let's watch the rest of the movies." Hector changed the subject.

He settled Steele on the couch with some decaffeinated coffee with skim milk and plain popcorn, no butter and very little salt. He put in the first movie. The boys were enthralled.

Felipe jumped up and down. "Do you see that R2D2 is giving Princess Leia the message?"

Matteo turned to his brother. "Felipe, sit down and don't talk. We can't hear the movie."

"I'm sorry." Felipe sat right down next to Steele and cuddled under his shoulder. Hector noticed that there was nary a sniffle. He wasn't as frightened as he was when he arrived.

After the first movie, it was time for a late lunch. Hector made tuna salad sandwiches with the low-fat mayonnaise he picked up the night before. He served the sandwiches with baked potato chips.

"This is what I have to eat?" Steele complained. "My stomach is going to think my throat's been cut."

"I have chicken noodle soup to go with the sandwiches and leftover brownies for the boys for dessert," Hector said. "Later on, you can cheat on your diet, but you had your heart attack on Friday and it's only Sunday, so it would behoove you to eat right for a few months.

"Dad, I looked it up on Grandma's computer. You need to go on a low-fat, low-salt diet. Grandma says we need the fat to develop our bodies, but you don't. We don't want you to be sick," Matteo said. "If you need us to do it, we'll all go on the diet."

Hector added, "A low-salt, low-fat diet would be good for me, too. We've been eating too well, and I've gained weight."

"There are special cookbooks for people with bad hearts. I found them on the web. I was going to tell Papa about them. I'd buy one, but unless I find someone I can do chores for, I have no money." Matteo took a bite of his sandwich. "This isn't bad, Dad. The mayonnaise is still creamy."

"You're going to get an allowance of ten dollars a week, and Felipe, because he is younger, will get five until he's ten years old like you." Hector smiled at Matteo's astonishment.

"You mean I get money for just being your kid and so does Felipe?"

"You get money for keeping your room clean, taking out the trash, doing well in school, and behaving yourself. If you don't do those things, we'll dock your allowance so you'll get less," Hector explained.

"I did all sorts of chores for *them* and I never got a penny. Are you sure? You don't have to give us money. I love it here even if I don't get an allowance."

Hector laughed. "I'm sure."

"Thank you, Dad, Papa." He whispered in Hector's ear, "Now I can buy Felipe something for Christmas and something for you and Dad, too."

Hector shook his head. "Matteo, the allowance is for you to buy things for yourself."

"Giving back would make me happy, and I have all the other weeks to buy stuff for myself. There are three weeks until Christmas. I'll have thirty dollars. If you would take me to Walmart, I can get a lot of things for thirty dollars. I know how to shop."

"Okay, little man." Hector tousled his hair. "Walmart, it is."

Felipe pulled on Hector's belt. "Can I go to Walmart with Matteo?"

"Yes, chipmunk, you can go, too." Hector laughed.

"What about me?" Steele whined. "You can't leave me by myself."

"I'll get one of the guys to keep you company. You don't get to go out of the house for two weeks unless you're going to the doctor's office." Hector made sure he looked stern.

Steele rolled his eyes.

"After two weeks, you can drive and we can—"

Steele hissed, "The boys are here."

"All go out to the movies to see the newest *Star Wars* picture."

Steele blushed.

"What did you think I was going to say?" Hector teased.

Steele gave him a lethal stare. "You know what I was talking about. It's in that damn pamphlet."

"Uh, we're finished. Can we be excused?" Matteo asked.

Hector nodded.

As the boys left the room, Felipe said, "Why did we have to leave? They were talking about the movies."

"Shush. I read the pamphlet and it wasn't about movies."

Steele turned to Hector and laughed.

Later Sunday Evening

Steele was reading in bed when Hector came back from Walmart with the missing school supplies. "You should be asleep," Hector scolded.

"I'm doing what I'm supposed to be doing and getting some rest. My feet are up and the only thing I'm holding is my Kindle. If you want me to sleep, come to bed. We have to be up early in the morning for the kids to go to school." Steele put down his Kindle.

"I'll go up to check on the boys, and then I'll be down to bed. Do you want some Caffeine-free Diet Coke?"

"Christ, I can't even have regular Coke?" Steele whined.

"I can give you ginger ale or 7Up, but since you like Coke, I bought the caffeine-free variety," Hector explained patiently. "Aren't the boys and I worth it?"

Steele sighed. "Of course you are. Yeah, bring me

a can and leave it on the nightstand in case I get thirsty. Kiss the boys for me." Hector left the room.

Yeah, Hector and the boys are worth this bullshit diet and anything else I have to do to keep them safe and happy.

Chapter Sixteen

Monday after Thanksgiving
Eight in the Morning

Hector could see the boys were nervous. Both boys picked at their food. "Come on now, you can't go to school on an empty stomach. I packed homemade subs for your lunch, with a bag of chips and an orange plus a bottle of water each."

"Thank you, Papa," Matteo said listlessly.

"What's wrong, son?" Hector watched Matteo's eyes fill up.

"Everyone is going to know what *he* did to me and why." A tear ran down Matteo's cheek.

"This is a new school. If someone knows, we'll deal with it. You be proud of who you are. Just tell them that your dad is a gay Special Agent for the FBI who runs the Albuquerque office, your papa is a gay sheriff, and you know a doctor, a nurse, and a DEA and FBI agent, all of whom are gay. Your brother is in kindergarten; you're in fifth grade. He's going to have to deal with the fact he has two daddies, and, next year, he'll have to deal with it on his own because you'll be going to middle school."

"How can I take care of Felipe if he's in a different school?" Matteo asked. "And what happens if the kids make fun of him because of me?"

"That's why I want to meet your teachers so that doesn't happen to either of you. Don't worry about the chipmunk. Dad and I will take care of both of you. If you have a hard time in this school, we'll send both of you to one of the secular academies. Look for the Garcia kids. I work with their dad. You've met Jose Garcia. He has two boys yours and Felipe's age. They won't be prejudiced. They know Dad and me. We play cards with Deputy Garcia."

Steele came into the kitchen. "What's for breakfast?"

"For you and me—turkey bacon and oatmeal. The boys are having oatmeal and regular bacon. We're all having some fruit salad. You can have two thousand six hundred calories a day because you don't need to lose weight. But you need to eat complex carbohydrates, ergo oatmeal." Hector handed out the plates.

"You're going inside the school with them?" Steele asked.

"Of course."

"I'm coming with you," Steele said adamantly.

"You're supposed to rest," Hector protested.

"It's a ten-minute ride, round trip. I'll get out of the car, walk fifty feet, go inside, meet the teachers, and then go home. If we're going to co-parent the boys, this is non-negotiable."

Hector let out a breath. "I'll call Dare and see if it's okay. Only because I know you'd follow me over and you're not supposed to drive." Hector tapped Dare's number into his cell phone.

"It's Hector. You're on speaker. Steele wants to go with me and the boys to meet their teachers for their first day at the new school."

"As long as he doesn't overexert himself, he can get out of the car, meet the teachers, get back into the car, and go home, nothing else. He had a heart attack a few days ago. He needs to rest or he won't get better."

Steele smiled at Hector in triumph. "Dare, I promise I won't do anything I'm not supposed to do. I just want the teachers to know the boys have two parents who care deeply about them."

"I'm letting you go because it's for the kids, but I want you home right after you drop them off and no more exertion today."

"Thanks, Dare. I'll make an appointment with the nutritionist today, and you can schedule the stress test at the end of the week."

"I'm holding you to that, Steele. I have no desire to lose a friend to heart disease when I'm a heart surgeon. I have to set you up with a cardiologist appointment, too. Dr. Huntsman is a good man. Call me when you get home and I'll give you the number."

"That's just your way of making sure I come right back."

Aden called out from the background, "He's sneaky that way."

***

Steele ate and got dressed. Soon they were all ready to go. They took Explorer with the Sheriff's Decal on the side. Steele chuckled. Hector was going to protect their boys by intimidation.

They were at the school in five minutes. After

their parent's trial, the boys would walk unless there was inclement weather, but for now, their Dad and Papa were going to drive them.

They signed in and spoke to the principal, Mr. Albright, who knew Hector because he was the sheriff. Hector addressed him, "These are my foster sons. Here is the paperwork from CYFD. Their parents are in jail, and, before that, they abused both boys. They cannot take them out of school; they are not allowed within three hundred yards of the kids. Here is a copy of the restraining order. No one but Steele, or I can take the kids from their classrooms. The one exception is Debra Schaeffer who will occasionally babysit. Here is a picture of her for you to keep on file. She's their unofficial grandma."

"I understand. Unfortunately, this is not the first case like this that the school has had to deal with. I'll quietly explain the situation to their teachers. Let's take them to their classes."

Steele interrupted. "Mr. Albright, Matteo may need tutoring. He had vision problems that weren't addressed and, as a result, had difficulty keeping up in class. He now has glasses and so does Felipe."

Mrs. Exton will be Matteo's teacher. I'll have her do an evaluation, and, if necessary, I'll recommend a tutor. Do you want to put him in a remedial class?"

"Hell no. If he needs a tutor, we'll hire one. But he's a pretty smart kid. Now that he's able to see, he'll catch up quickly."

The principal looked over Matteo's records. "Even with his vision problems, he got Bs and Cs. I think you're right. He'll catch up with a little bit of extra help. Felipe is going to Mrs. Anderson's class. She knows how to handle frightened and troubled kids." Principal Albright looked at Felipe, who was hiding behind Matteo and Hector.

"They haven't had positive experiences with school. I want to make sure that changes," Hector said firmly.

"I'll make sure it does," the principal promised. "Let's take the boys to meet their teachers and classmates."

At each class, Hector and Steele introduced themselves to the teacher, handed the boys their lunches and backpacks, and kissed them good-bye.

"I'll pick you up at four," Hector told them.

"Okay, Papa. Dad, you be careful. We'll see you when we get home."

***

The two new fathers pulled into the garage. "That went well. They are both in classes with the Garcia boys. They're good kids, and Jose asked them to look out for Felipe and Matteo. From what I understand, the Garcias are very involved with the school and the kids are popular. They'll be good friends for the boys to have." They came into the house through the garage door.

"I'm warning you," Hector told Steele as they went to sit in the kitchen, "I intend us to be very hands-on parents. We're joining the PTA, we're going on school trips, and we're volunteering to be class parents."

"My mom did that for me. It always helped. I don't object to doing that, and, as head of the division, I can make my own hours unless we have an unusually hot case." Steele got up and fetched himself a can of his new diet soda.

"There are two of us. We can make this work. But

you're home for the next six weeks. We'll follow the cardiologist's instructions and see where we are after that. I have to call Beatrice and let her know what happened. She should find out from us, not someone else." Hector picked up his cell.

***

To Steele's relief, the call to Beatrice went well.

"As long as the damage is minimal, there should be no problem. We have a dearth of foster parents for gay kids and especially gay kids with siblings. Sometimes we have to split them up, so a family willing to take both of them goes a long way toward getting approval," she told them.

"How are things going with the termination of those bastards' parental rights?"

"That's not going to be as easy. We have them now on attempting to shoot Matteo and Edwards and actually managing to shoot Matteo while out on bail. Bail was revoked, but they still have to have their day in court."

"Shouldn't the pictures and the shooting be enough?" Hector was annoyed.

"We need a conviction on both the abuse and the drug charges before we can start the process. Remember, innocent until proven guilty." Steele heard her tapping her pencil on her desk.

"Right now I can prove abuse. But many a parent gets away with it by going into rehab for their drug habit and taking parenting classes. If we can put them in prison for possession with intent to distribute the drugs and attempting to get Matteo to sell them at school, we'll be in better shape. Tell Mr. Rivers he needs an airtight case against them."

"He has one," Hector said grimly. "Unfortunately, Matteo was a witness to the drug operation and will have to testify, especially since he was the one to report his parents in the first place. And they can't get away with saying they didn't know about the drugs under the floor and in the walls because Matteo knew exactly where to tell the DEA to look.

"Both the DEA and our office are pushing for speedy trials. The DA said he'd take a plea for thirty years and they can get out in twenty with good behavior. The charges will bring them over sixty years if we have to go to trial and win a conviction."

"So, hopefully, the kids will be emancipated before their parents ever leave federal or state prison," Hector said.

"Even if they go to prison, unless we get the right judge, they may not terminate the parents' rights. I'm going to talk to the district attorney about making sure this goes to the right judge. Neither one of those boys should be forced to live with those people. I'm not supposed to take sides, but with a case when the abuse is as severe as this one, I can't remain neutral. I have a responsibility to those boys." Beatrice sighed. "It's never easy."

"We're documenting all of the neglect, from their refusal to take the kids to the eye doctor when it was plain Matteo had a problem with his vision to the missing vaccinations and basic clothing. They had money in the bank. Rivers seized their accounts with the help of the drug laws. They had the money to take care of the kids, even if it was drug money. They just chose not to." Steele was indignant.

"I can tell you're working up a good head of steam, Mr. Adams. Not a good idea for someone who just had a heart attack. Let Rivers and I do our jobs. The kids are staying with you. As soon as you have the physical, that will be my recommendation."

Steele mouthed, "Thank God," to Hector.

"Thank you for helping us do this. We already love the boys, and I think they care about us." Hector got up from his chair. "I'll let you go do your job. We'll take good care of them."

"I'm sure you will." With that Beatrice hung up.

"I can't believe those bastards can get the kids back with rehab and a few parenting classes after shooting one of them," Steele fumed.

"Take it easy. You can't afford the stress right now. Let's think about Christmas and start ordering their presents. The mailman's going to love us."

They went into the great room and sat on the couch, and Hector brought over his computer.

"What are we going to do about the money? We were going to go to the bank and open a joint account today." Steele was obsessing.

"We both bank at New Mexico Bank and Trust. I'll explain the situation to the manager. I'll empty my account into yours and bring home the signature cards to change it to a joint account. In the meanwhile, my Amazon account is linked directly to my American Express. We can buy everything we need and take care of the bill at the end of the month by which time we should have the accounts commingled."

"I want us to get married as soon as I can reasonably leave the house. We'll have Aden and Dare as witnesses and the boys at the wedding in front of a judge, the sooner the better. I need to contact my lawyer about changing my will." Steele started to make a list.

"We need a marriage license. There is no wait in New Mexico, so we can get married as soon as we obtain the license. Are you sure you don't want Sanchez, Rivers, Debra, and my deputies to come?"

"I'd rather do it quietly and without fanfare, just the boys and our witnesses unless you want your family to come."

"No, my family can find out later when the situation with the boys is stable. I don't want them to make trouble with their bigotry."

"After we get approval from Beatrice, we can have a party. By that time, I should be in better shape." Steele grimaced. "Of all the times my body could pick to let me down, this was the worst."

"Don't stress. With our friends' help, the boys will have a wonderful Christmas, and, in three weeks, you should be in pretty good shape to celebrate the holiday and a January wedding. Now, let's start pointing and clicking. Both boys told Santa they wanted lightsabers so that means *Star Wars* toys will be a big hit." Hector brought his computer up.

"What do we have so far?" Steele asked.

"Sports equipment, a football, baseballs, bats, gloves, and helmets for baseball as well as for their bikes. At Best Buy, I picked up computers, phones, and headphones. We'll get the Kindles from Amazon. I debated buying iPods, but their phones have a music function. The phones are pretty basic. Actually, Rivers and Sanchez sprang for the phones. They're going to say Santa left some things at their house because there wasn't enough room in the sleigh. Dare, Aden, and Debra are all telling the same story." Hector went to the Amazon website.

"We should buy the Kindles and load them with books. I want the kids to read. We'll have to see what they like." Steele perused the website. "The Kindle Fire should do nicely for both boys. You can listen to audio books too with that model which will be good for Felipe." Hector put quantity two in the box and used one click to purchase the Kindles.

"Let's search for what toys they have for Star Wars. Here, they have the Millennium Falcon. Let's get that and some action figures. They can play with that together. It says four years old and up," Steele suggested. He glanced at the usually bought together items and nodded at the computer. "And here are the lightsabers."

"I also like the R2D2 that takes commands. That should be Matteo's. We'll get the one recommended for ages three to fifteen for Felipe. For their stockings, we can get Felipe the stickers, a coloring book and crayons, and books, and Matteo some books." Steel clicked, and Hector spotted something else.

"That Command Star Destroyer looks good for them to share, and it has more action figures. We should get as many action figures as we can find, and put them in their stockings. That puts the imagination back in play, also, a matchbox racetrack and cars. They would enjoy that." Hector went to that page.

"This summer I want to get a tree house and a jungle gym. We'll put special padding underneath the monkey bars. We need to find out their birthdays. I don't want them to be forgotten for anything anymore."

"Those should be in the paperwork Beatrice gave us. Let's look now." They got up and read the work-up sheet. Felipe was in May on the fifteenth. Matteo, July; far enough from Christmas that they'd get nice gifts instead of one extra Christmas gift held back."

"Rivers said that Matteo should have a skateboard. A cheap one at first until we see if he likes it. Did you get clothing?" Steele asked.

"I picked up five outfits each at Penny's. Debra's going to buy clothes. We need to make a list of what we have and send it to our friends. Then there will be no duplication. Tell them not to buy Star Wars stuff because we just bought out the store." Steele chuckled.

Hector asked, "How about some roller blades for both boys?"

"Good idea. Let's see what they have." Steele did a search. They found some they liked and bought them.

"How about decorations for their rooms. I see two different *Star Wars* sheet and comforter sets. Both come with café curtains. And they have wall stickers to decorate the room. Let's get them those lifelike Fathead decals for the walls. They have a selection of *Star Wars* themed Fatheads," Hector pointed out.

"We have to build some shelves and get two toy boxes. We can also put posters on the wall. I think we better stop now. As much as I want to buy them everything, we can't, or we'll spoil them." Steele sighed.

The poker game is Tuesday this week. Garcia's hosting, and we can bring the boys. As soon as this stuff arrives, we have to wrap it while they're in school. You get wrapping duty; you'll be home. I'll take care of the tree. I need the key to your storage locker to get the decorations."

Steele took the key from his keychain and handed it to Hector. "They're right up front, you know, last in, first out. I can get the guys to help me get the stuff and the tall ladder. I'll call Sanchez and Rivers."

"I'll call Rivers and Sanchez. You're getting nothing out of storage. Four to six weeks, remember. The cardiologist has to sign off before you start climbing ladders and hauling boxes. Right now, you have a ten-pound limit. Let's not push the envelope."

Chapter Seventeen

Hector got up from the couch. "I'm going to make some decaf. Do you want some?"

Steele followed him into the kitchen and sat at the table. "Yes, thanks. What are you going to do about taking the boys to and from school if I can't drive for two weeks? You have to go to work, and Dare claims I can't do much for at least that amount of time."

Hector measured out the water and the coffee. "I didn't get a chance to tell you. I applied for paid family leave for three months starting immediately. Garcia told me I qualified because we just became parents. It's departmental policy. You're going back to work before I am."

"I should have Sanchez check to see if the FBI has the same benefit. I'll take the three months, even if the leave is unpaid. I'd feel better if the boys have both of us here."

Hector sat next to Steele. "I trust Debra, but at least one of us should be home with them and armed at all times until those monsters they called parents and their cohorts are securely in prison for the next twenty or more years." Hector drummed his fingers on the table in annoyance.

"We also have to worry that those bastards may have associates who are out on bail and pissed off at Matteo for exposing their operation, although Rivers said he'd try to keep Matteo's name out of it." Steele gritted his teeth.

"I'm glad I answered that call and the boys are with us. It's like they were fated to be ours. Someone else may not appreciate the danger their parents presented. Someone else would have let Matteo go to a group home." Hector heard the pot stop dripping and got up to pour the coffee.

Hector put back the pot and Steele grabbed his hand, and kissed his wrist. "I'm glad you took that call. It solidified our relationship as well as gave us two great kids. If I weren't in love with you already, I would have fallen for you for fostering those two boys. Shit, I'm getting sappy."

Hector blinked, wiped at his eyes, and turned to the refrigerator and changed the subject. "I'll make us turkey sandwiches with lettuce and tomato for lunch on Kaiser rolls. I bought low-fat mayo, but you could make it into a sub by using olive oil and vinegar."

"Sounds good. What can I have with it?" Steele raised his brow.

"I have baked potato chips and coleslaw. For dinner, I'm picking up a nice piece of salmon when I go to pick up the boys, which you can have with a white wine and lemon sauce and brown and wild rice with peas."

"When did you start cooking that fancy?" Disbelief shown on Steele's face.

"I looked up heart healthy recipes on the net and found out how to make it because I know you won't stay on your diet if the food doesn't taste good." Hector took a sip of his coffee. "Not bad for decaf."

"Will the kids eat fish?" Steele wondered.

"They haven't refused anything we've served them so far." Hector swallowed some coffee. "You're right. This coffee isn't so bad. Since we can't make love...." He arched his eyebrow at Steele.

"Let's wrap Christmas presents. You got wrapping paper, ribbon, stickers, tape, and tags when you went out with Sanchez and Rivers, didn't you?" Steele finished his coffee.

"Yeah, I had to make sure you had something to do that wasn't strenuous." Hector laughed.

"I hope you got wrapping paper for kids and not fancy foil. That stuff rips really easily."

"I got Christmas superheroes, *Star Wars*, and Christmas cartoon characters. For our presents and the ones we're giving our friends, I got mistletoe and Christmas trees. Does that pass muster?" Hector asked in exasperation. Steele was never happy unless he thought he was running the show. Hector liked being the power behind the throne, but sometimes it got ridiculous.

"They have *Star Wars* wrapping paper for Christmas?" Steele asked with skepticism.

"Not really, but I thought the kids would like it even if it wasn't Christmas wrap." Hector defended himself. "Besides, it came in big rolls and we have a lot of big presents to wrap. I also bought cloth ribbons and that rustic string. I like the presents to look nice."

"I do, too. I'll help you get the packages," Steele offered.

"No, they are in the ceiling of the garage. I have to climb the small ladder. I'll bring them down and hand them to you and you can carry them to the great room. They're all less than ten pounds." Hector opened the ladder and put it at the beginning of the plywood section.

"Okay, I don't like it, but I suppose if I want to stay around for you, Matteo, and the chipmunk, I have to play by the rules."

Hector brought down half of the presents, and they spent the morning wrapping. Steele stored the wrapped presents under their bed and in their closets. "We have to tell them that if the door to our bedroom is closed, they're not to go inside. In an emergency, they can shout our name or knock."

"Good idea. In two weeks, that rule is going to come in pretty handy." Hector leered. "Let me make lunch, and then you can nap until it's time to get the boys from school. I promise I won't go without you."

***

Hector touched Steele's shoulder and kissed his forehead. "It's three-thirty. The kids get out at four."

"How long was I out?" Steele yawned.

"We finished lunch at one and you went to bed at one-thirty, so you had your required two- hour nap. Get up and dressed. We have to leave in ten minutes. I don't want to be too far back in the line to pick them up. They might get nervous."

Hector and Steele were the fourth in line when the kids came out. Matteo was holding Felipe's hand. They saw Hector's Explorer right away, and the two of them came running to the car.

Felipe was chattering as they climbed in. Matteo fastened his brother's seat belt then his own.

"My teacher is so nice. She sat me next to Jorge

Garcia. He said he knows you, Papa," Felipe said.

"Yes, you've met his dad. He's my deputy," Hector reminded him.

"What about you, Matteo?" Steele asked. "How was your first day?"

"The teacher was nice, and Jose Garcia introduced me to everyone. I think I like him. My teacher was willing to help me catch up if I come to school an hour early every day until I am where the other kids are. I want to do well so you're proud of me."

"Don't ever worry about us being proud of you. We already are. You are a loving, responsible boy."

"Felipe can come early, too, because they have a Head Start program for the kids of those parents who have to go to work early. Since *they* wouldn't let him go to Pre-K maybe he could use the help." Matteo was looking out for his brother again.

"Would you like that, chipmunk, to go to school early to catch up to the other kids?" Hector turned onto Sandoval Drive. In two minutes, they were home. They pulled into the garage.

"Yes, I like school. This class is so much better. They don't make fun of my clothes or talk in whispers about *them*. I told all the other kids that Hector was my papa and Steele was my dad. There is a girl in my class that has two moms, so I don't stick out." Their chipmunk chattered on.

Hector was more concerned about Matteo's experience. Steele must have read his mind.

"You said your teacher is nice, Matteo? Were the kids kind?" Steele asked.

"I told the kids I was gay. I wanted to tell them right away so they didn't find out in a bad way. Most of them didn't care, and Jose made sure that those who did didn't bother me. It was really okay. I was frightened it wouldn't be." Matteo gave his fathers a little smile.

"They liked my *Star Wars* backpack. Did they like yours, Matteo?"

"Everyone asked where I got it. I said I didn't know because my Papa got it for me."

Hector unfastened his seat belt and everyone followed him into the house.

"You can tell them I got it on Amazon.com. I have a Prime membership so it was delivered in two days."

"Everyone wanted to look, and they thought it was neat that we watched the first six Star Wars movies. I told them that we're going to see number seven sometime after Christmas."

"It sounds like you did okay. Do you have homework?" Steele asked.

"Both of us do. I can help Felipe, if you're too busy," Matteo offered.

"No, son," Hector said. "I'll help Felipe, and Dad can help you. How does that sound?"

"Neat."

"Now you can have milk and cookies for your snack, and we'll hit the books. Okay?"

"We get a snack? Did you hear that Felipe? We get a snack when we come home." Matteo threw his arms around first Hector then Steele. "You're the best. We are very lucky boys."

"And we are very lucky parents."

Wednesday after Thanksgiving
Six in the Morning

"Get out of bed, Matteo. Grandma's coming to get us to make Santa's cookies today."

Matteo opened one eye and looked at the clock. "It's only six. Grandma won't be here until ten. We have to let Dad rest. If we get up, he will. Let's go to the other bedroom and quietly watch TV until we smell the coffee. Then we'll know someone is awake."

***

"They're awake." Hector opened his eyes. It took a few moments for him to register what Steele was trying to tell him.

First he panicked. "Are you okay? Does your chest hurt? I'll call 911!"

"Hold on, I'm good. I just wanted to tell you the kids are awake. They're trying to be quiet, but I keep hearing Matteo telling Felipe to shush." Steele chuckled.

"Did you get enough sleep?" Hector grumbled.

"It's seven now, and I went to bed at nine. I think ten hours constitutes enough sleep, don't you?" Steele's blue eyes sparkled.

"I'll get up and make the coffee." Hector started to get out of bed.

"No, you don't. I want some serious cuddling." Steele pulled on Hector's arm.

"That's going to lead to a place we can't go for another nine days," Hector told him, kissing his lips and reaching for his robe.

"Get back in this bed or I swear I'll drive to Denver. I'm not stupid. I know making love is a bad idea right now. I don't know if I could get it up anyway with the prescription Dare wrote, but cuddling is legal."

"Okay, you big lug." Hector got back into bed. "Come to Papa." He opened his arms to Steele.

Steele crawled into Hector's arms. "Before the boys came and you and I were still playing head games with one another, I always dreamed of waking up in your arms. I got to do that, even if it was only for a short time, and now I miss it."

"I suppose we're adult enough to cuddle without sex, God knows teenagers do it all the time and they're ruled by their hormones. Besides, I miss having your arms around me, too," Hector confessed.

The two men lay content for another half hour. Hector moved first. "I hear rumbling upstairs. You go make the coffee. I'll know if you don't use the decaf, so don't cheat. I'll go upstairs and see what they're doing."

Before he had a chance to move, someone knocked on their door.

"Papa, Dad, it's cookie day," their little chipmunk chattered."

"We'll be right out. Remember, our bedroom is off-limits," Hector said as he put on his pants.

"We remember," Matteo said.

Hector heard whispers. "They can't be doing *that*. The pamphlet said not for two weeks."

Hector started to laugh. Steele said, "What's so funny?"

"Matteo apparently read *all* of the pamphlet." Hector continued to chuckle. "Especially the part about Viagra and Cialis."

Steele blushed. "I wonder if I should have gotten him those glasses," he muttered.

It took only five minutes for both men to throw on sweats and they were out the door and into the kitchen where the boys sat at the table.

Felipe was wiggling. "What time is Grandma coming again?"

"She said she'd be here at ten." Hector answered. "What do you want for breakfast?"

"Can we have scrambled eggs, bacon, and English muffins?" Felipe asked.

"Is that okay with you, Matteo?" Hector watched him nod.

"The mailman is going to hate us today." Hector put eight eggs and milk into a bowl and whisked them together.

"Why is that?" Steele asked as he fried the bacon.

"Three words—two-day delivery," Hector answered. Steele cracked up.

"I'm getting eggs today?" Steele asked.

"Yes, I did a bit of reading last night and eggs don't significantly increase the amount of cholesterol in the blood when eaten in moderation. So, today, you can have eggs, but no bacon unless you want the turkey bacon." Hector slid the eggs into the skillet and turned the boys' bacon.

"I'm glad we're seeing the nutritionist on Friday, then *I'll* know what I can eat," Steele said archly.

"Don't forget you have your stress test right after your appointment with the dietician." Hector plated breakfast while Steele poured the juice and coffee. Hector also served cantaloupe. Steele raised an eyebrow. "Fruits and vegetable are good for you, the kids, and me."

"Is Grandma giving us our lunch?" Hector noticed that Matteo was always concerned about Felipe getting enough to eat. He grimaced at the idea of how many times the boys had gone hungry.

"Yes, Grandma's making you lunch, and Grandma is a very good cook, just like Uncle Aden."

"Are you going to stay with Dad, Papa?" Matteo looked concerned at the idea that Steele could be in the house alone.

"Don't worry, I'll be here. You go and have a good time at Grandma's house. When you finish eating, go get washed and dressed and you can watch television until Grandma comes to get you." Hector took the empty plates. The boys had inhaled their food. "Does anyone want more eggs?"

Matteo glanced at Felipe who shook his head. "No, Papa, we're good." Matteo herded Felipe back up the stairs.

Chapter Eighteen

Friday, Two Weeks after Black Friday

"You can get dressed now, Mr. Adams. You did well on your stress test last week, and, from what I understand, you're following your diet. Your cholesterol numbers look good, and your triglycerides are coming along nicely." Dr. Huntsman put his stethoscope back around his neck.

"May I begin to drive, Doctor?" Steele slipped on his T-shirt.

"You can drive, but, for the first week, I'd prefer you didn't drive alone. You may also resume sexual activities. It's a myth that gay sex is more strenuous than heterosexual sex. Speaking as a gay man, I can tell you not to go overboard and pound your partner into the mattress. That's the same advice I would give a heterosexual couple, but normal sexual activity may be resumed."

Steele chuckled, thinking of Matteo and the pamphlet. "Thank you, Doctor."

"You are a very lucky man that your partner knew enough to give you an aspirin as soon as you started to experience chest pain. I'm writing prescriptions for you to stay on the four medications Dr. Rourke gave you when he discharged you from the hospital, and I want to see you in four weeks unless you have any pain or discomfort before then. I'm giving you a prescription for nitroglycerin. If you feel pressure in your chest, take one immediately and call 911."

Steele resumed dressing, putting on the Stamford sweatshirt he'd bought as an undergraduate studying pre-law. "Is there anything I should avoid? Climbing stairs, ladders...." Steele leaned over and tied his sneakers.

"I'd take it easy on the stairs, no more than twice a day, and I'd avoid ladders for another few weeks. But six weeks after your attack, after our next appointment, you should be able to resume all of your normal activities." The doctor made a few notes on his electronic pad.

Steele got serious. "Can I do any exercise? If I don't, I'll gain weight, which won't be good for my heart or my relationship."

The doctor laughed. "Considering the lengths to which your partner went to save you, I doubt a few pounds will make a difference."

"I'm ten years older than he is. I have to keep up." Steele groaned.

"I doubt that. Talk to him about it. If you don't communicate, you'll be stressed, and I don't want you stressed out. He loved you before the attack. He'll love you after it. You'll be almost as good as new by the end of six weeks. As Dr. Rourke told you, you have minimal damage."

"I can't help worrying about things. Hector, the boys, their criminal parents," Steele muttered.

"Worry about disaster when it happens, not before. Do you need to see a psychologist? Some people do when they find out they're no longer invincible."

"No, I've accepted that I have to go easier if I wish to stay around for my family. I have two boys now who depend on Hector and me."

"That's why I want you to walk for exercise. You need to increase the amount of time you walk gradually. Walking is an aerobic exercise. Gradually increase the time you walk until you hit sixty minutes a day. Talk to me before you resume strength training, spinning, or the rowing machine. As a matter of fact, just do the walking until I see you again. Don't push it. If you're out of breath, stop."

"I find I'm tired, even if I take my nap," Steele complained.

"You may still experience fatigue as a side effect of the medication, but that's normal. However, if you find yourself constantly fighting sleep, come in to see me. Any other questions?" The doctor moved toward the door.

"Wait. Can I lift more than ten pounds? My five-year-old loves to be picked up. He's our foster son and came from an abusive environment and the social worker says that affection shows Felipe that he's wanted." Steele buckled his belt.

"For the time being, he can sit on your lap to cuddle, but a five-year-old can weigh as much as forty pounds, so no lifting him off the floor yet. I'll see you in four weeks."

Steele finished dressing and went out to the waiting room where Hector was pacing the floor. "What did he say?"

"I can drive, but you have to drive with me for

another week. We can have sex so long as I don't try to and I quote, 'pound you into the mattress.' He gave me a prescription for nitroglycerin tablets in case I get chest pain, but my numbers are good. I have to stay on my diet, and he'll see me in four weeks. I have to work up to walking sixty minutes a day and still can't lift, reach, or strain. I'm to stop whatever I'm doing if I get short of breath. Basically, except for the walking and driving, my physical activity is still limited. I'll need another stress test to be completely in the clear." Steele sighed.

"Has the diet helped?" Hector asked as they waited for the elevator.

"Yes, between the diet and the medication, my numbers are good. So I gradually increase my physical activity, except for the lifting, until I see him next. You have to buy me Raisin Bran and whole oat cereal for breakfast. Dr. Huntsman says you can get a good whole oat flake cereal at Trader Joe's."

They stepped onto the elevator, and Hector tossed Steele the keys to the Navigator. "Let's go pick up the kids."

***

"Dad, you're driving. Does that mean you're all better?" Felipe clambered into the Navigator.

"Not all better, chipmunk, but getting there. I still can't pick you up yet, but you can sit on my lap and cuddle. I have to watch what I eat, and I need to take walks every day."

"Matteo and I can go for walks with you." Felipe spoke like he didn't want to let Steele out of his sight. "Right, Matteo, we can go with Dad, can't we?" Steele could see Matteo nod in the rearview mirror.

"Dad can also go up and down the steps twice a day. That means he can come up and kiss you good night." Hector asked, "Are you in your booster seat, Felipe?"

Matteo checked his brother's seat belt then fastened his own. "I'm glad you bought Felipe a booster seat; he's too short for a regular seat belt."

"Once we saw that the seat belt didn't hit him in the right place, your Papa went out and bought one right away. Papa is a sheriff and has seen too many accidents not to err on the side of safety." Steele smiled at his partner.

"Dad, what's err?"

"Err means to make a mistake. Not to err is not to make a mistake. Papa wants to keep you safe. So if he makes an error, he'd rather make a mistake trying to keep you too safe than not safe enough." Steele put the Navigator in gear and followed the other cars out to Chayote Road to drive the mile home from the school.

"When do you go back to the doctor, Dad?" Matteo was obviously worried.

"I go back the second week in January."

"Can you still help us put up the tree?" That was the closest Steele ever heard Matteo come to whining.

"I can help put up the lights and the ornaments, but I can't climb a ladder. So Papa will have to put the lights on top of the tree and hang those ornaments. All of your adopted uncles are going to help. I can go with you guys to pick out the tree, though. We'll go to get it next Friday. You have to use my computer and research what kind of tree you want."

"What kind of trees are there?" Matteo asked, curious.

"I know what kind they had in California. I don't know what kinds you have here. Ask Papa. But I'll bet they have one with long needles and one with short."

"How are we going to get it home, Dad?" Felipe, who had been unusually quiet, asked.

"Uncle Jerry has volunteered to help lift it and tie it on top of the Navigator and help Papa put in a bucket of water in the yard. We'll put on the lights a few days before Christmas, and we'll do the ornaments and the ribbon garland on Christmas Eve. Does that sound good? Everything is going to be exactly the same as it was before my heart attack. The only difference is that we'll eat more nutritious meals and I'll be walking instead of lifting weights."

"Yessssssss. Can we have cookies and eggnog when we put up the tree? Grandma says it's traditional."

"Of course. Uncle Aden is going to bring food. Papa will make the eggnog, and Grandma already made the cookies which we have stored in the big freezer. We're all set to go. We have everything we need for Santa to come."

"At the mall, when we visited him, he said he won't lose our address or forget us this year. You think I'm a good boy, Dad, don't you?" Felipe asked with trepidation.

"You and Matteo are the best boys ever. There will be no coal in your stockings. That's how you tell if Santa thinks you've been a bad boy; you get coal in your stocking." Steele pulled into the garage.

"Do we have stockings to hang?" Matteo asked with some skepticism.

"As a matter of fact, you do. Your stockings are knitted with your name on them in sequins. I'll show you when we get home. Grandma made them. Uncle

Aden and Uncle Dare have the same ones." Hector got out of the car and opened the back door.

"Do you and Dad have stockings to hang?" Felipe's squeaky voice asked as he scurried out of the car.

"We do, just not the same kind that you have." Hector turned off the alarm.

"Why not?" their chipmunk asked.

"Because Grandma only had time to make two. She made Uncle Aden's when he was little, and she made Uncle Dare's before you came to live with us."

Felipe seemed to consider his papa's answer. "Okay, but maybe Grandma can make you special stockings next year. I'll ask her," he decided.

Matteo spoke up as they put their backpacks on the table. "No, you won't. Grandma's done enough, and she may have other things to do. If she has time to make Dad and Papa a stocking, she will. If she doesn't, they already have two to use."

"Put your coats away and put on your play clothes. Dad will make you a snack." The kids ran up the stairs.

Matteo came back down. "Papa, which clothes are our play clothes?"

"The ones from Walmart. I don't care if they get damaged."

"Okay, Papa."

Steele took out the vegetables and dip they'd made earlier and poured each boy a glass of apple juice. He shouted up the stairs, "After snacks, it's homework before you go upstairs to play and watch television."

Matteo came bounding down the stairs. "I have math homework. Can you help me, Dad?"

"I'll try. They do math different now than they

did when I was a kid. I read your textbook, and I think I see what they're doing, but if I can't help, we'll get someone who can."

"Okay, Dad."

"I have my letters to practice, some spelling words, and a book to read from the library. It's my turn to read aloud on Monday, so I have to practice." Felipe was still chattering. "Can you help me with that, Papa?"

"Sure, chipmunk. Come sit by me. First, have your snack, and, after, that we'll do homework."

The boys were happily munching on their carrots and cucumber spears when the phone rang. Steele got up to answer.

"It's Sanchez. Let me talk to Gomez."

Steele shrugged. "It's Sanchez. He wants to talk to you." Steele handed the phone to Hector.

***

"Are the kids with you?" Jerry asked.

"Yeah, they just came home from school and are having their snacks and about to start homework."

"Don't put the phone on speaker."

"Okay." Steele raised an eyebrow, and Hector shook his head.

"Their mother just hung herself in her cell, and when the father heard, he overcame a guard and took his gun. Rivers and Garcia are on their way over there. I'm about two minutes out. Put the kids in an inside bathroom and stay away from the windows. Get out your guns."

"Right away." Hector hung up the phone.

"Steele, go get our weapons from the gun safe. Matteo, take your brother and get into the bathtub in the upstairs bathroom with no windows. Now!"

Matteo grabbed Felipe by the hand and ran up the stairs. Steele came back with their Glock 22s and 40 caliber bullets. "It's that bastard, isn't it? He's escaped."

"Once she realized she faced at best twenty years in prison and at worst sixty, she hung herself with a bedsheet. When he heard, he knocked out a guard, and Sanchez thinks he's headed here. He has nothing to lose."

"What are they doing about it?"

"The Rio Rancho police, the sheriff's department, the DEA, and the FBI are all on their way, about two minutes out. We need to hold until then. He stole the guard's twenty-two. Stay away from the windows." Hector's countenance was grim. "No heroics unless the kids are in imminent danger."

"I'll take the front; you take the back. We alarmed the perimeter after the last time. I'm turning on the alarm now. We don't have time to vacate the property." Steele was grim.

"They think he's headed straight here, and he has a department vehicle and uniform. Until you can see their face, don't shoot at anyone from the sheriff's department. I'm getting my hunting rifles with the telescopes out of the gun cabinet in the bedroom."

The perimeter alarm went off. A bullet whizzed by Hector's head. "Drop!" he yelled at Steele."

Hector heard the sirens and Pena's shouts. "I'm going to get those little bastards no matter what you do. Rosa is dead because of those two."

Hector shouted out the window, "Rosa is dead because of you and your drugs, not the kids. Give yourself up. You'll get twenty on a plea bargain. If you persist in this, you'll get life without parole and prison isn't kind to child killers."

Another bullet broke the glass in the kitchen window. Suddenly, several shots rang out from outside the house. Steele got up from his crouch and watched Pena fall. "He's dead," he heard Sanchez shout.

Rivers came to the door and knocked. "It's Jon. Could you turn off the alarm? He's dead, but we still have to call a bus."

Hector carefully opened the door, punching in the code for the alarm. Rivers came in the house. "One of my agents got him. He tried to wing him, but he turned and the shot went to his heart. It's almost funny that Matteo turned and was saved and this bastard turned and got it in the heart. The Special Agent in Charge of my division witnessed the shooting. It was a good shoot, but we still have to go through the motions. Keep the kids inside until the bus leaves then take them out to dinner. CSI has to retrieve the two bullets from the scene. We'll also call a glass company to put in an emergency window."

Chapter Nineteen

Friday Evening

They went to McDonalds, where Steele was able to have a salad while the kids ate burgers. Hector stayed in the car to call Beatrice.

Steele began, "I have some news for the two of you."

"We have to leave because he came again. I heard the shots," Matteo said, resigned, as tears began to pour down his cheeks. He put his arm around his brother who got hysterical.

"Easy, easy. You never have to leave if you don't want to go. What I have to say is I'm sorry to tell you that both of your parents died today. Your mother hung herself in her jail cell and your father escaped and tried to shoot Papa through the kitchen window. One of Uncle Jon's people tried to shoot him in the arm to make him drop the gun, but he turned and was hit in the heart."

The boys took a few minutes to consider what Steele told them then Matteo sighed in relief. "You can stop crying, Felipe. They can never hurt us again."

"Is Santa not going to come because I'm glad they're gone?" Felipe asked.

"No, chipmunk. Santa is coming to our house. Do you want to be our real sons?"

"Oh yes, Dad, please, if you want us."

"We want you. Papa is out in the car calling Mrs. Marks about the paperwork."

***

"Beatrice, if you've been watching the news, you know what happened," Hector said, his voice indicating how nervous he was. They couldn't lose the boys.

"Yes, I was just going to call you." Hector could hear Beatrice's pencil tapping on her desk pad. That usually happened when she was upset.

"I swear, Beatrice, neither one of us fired our guns. We put the boys in the tub in the upstairs bathroom without the windows. They were never in danger."

"Who shot him?" Beatrice asked.

"One of River's DEA agents did it, but it was a good shoot. We never had the chance to fire our guns."

"That's good because it would complicate things. Do you still want to adopt the boys?" Beatrice asked.

"Of course," Hector snapped at her.

"Easy, Hector, I had to ask. There will be more paperwork and background checks. The process will take six months. I'll still get Steele certified as a foster parent. That will make it easier for the adoption. But I've already searched for relatives. There are none. So the path is clear."

"Can I tell the boys that they will be ours in six months?"

"Will you two be married by then? It will make things easier."

"We'll get married next Monday. The kids only have half days of school next week because of the holiday, and we want them at the wedding.

"I'll get the paperwork started."

Hector hung up the phone and called Garcia. "Is the circus almost done?"

"Rivers can't get the glazers in until tomorrow. Are you willing to pay Saturday rates?"

"I'll pay whatever it takes. Have the crime scene people cleaned up and found the two bullets?"

"They found them in the kitchen wall. The bullets are going to ballistics. They took your and Steele's guns to check for residue just to eliminate you as the shooters. River's guy, Walsh, already claimed the shot."

"How long before we can take the boys home?"

"You'll be good in about an hour. I'm boarding up the kitchen window until tomorrow. The glazer will be there at ten."

***

Steele didn't want to admit it, but he was scared of what Beatrice would do because of the shooting. It was, after all, the second one. Even if the boys had to go somewhere else for only a few days, they would be traumatized. He looked toward the door and saw Hector making his way inside.

Shaking slightly, Steele arched an eyebrow.

"Beatrice is continuing to vet you as a foster parent but is starting the process for adoption.

Adoption will take six months, more classes, more background checks, fingerprinting, and home visits. However, she's recommending the boys be placed with us. To facilitate this process, we're getting married next Monday so the boys can be there after their morning in school."

Steele was dumbstruck.

"What? You already proposed. I just set the date. We already decided against a big wedding, only the kids, Aden, and Dare. I'll call Judge Richardson and make an appointment. I did him a favor last year. He'll marry us in his chambers. We can get the license while the kids are in school Monday. I'll even let you drive."

Steele blushed. "I already have the rings." He looked at Hector then at the boys. "Since Santa doesn't come for adults, I bought them for us for Christmas."

"You're getting married and we can come? Does this mean Mrs. Marks said we can stay forever?" Matteo asked with trepidation.

"Yes, as long as Papa and I pass their tests for prospective parents and Beatrice gives the okay. What did she say?" Steele temporized.

"She says all she has to do is the paperwork. She's recommending the kids stay with us permanently. It will take six months for it to be official, but the boys are ours."

"We don't have to worry anymore? They're dead, and Mrs. Marks is going to let us stay?" Matteo was in tears.

"Stop crying." The chipmunk finally asserted himself. "Santa's coming in two weeks, and he knows where we live. We're warm, we have enough to eat, and you don't have to take care of me. Dad and Papa do. You don't have to cry anymore." Felipe hugged his brother.

"Are Dare and Aden off-shift?" Hector asked Steele.

"They're generally home by five. It's five now. Do you want me to call them?"

"Well, someone has to tell them they're playing best men on their day off." Hector bent over and gave each of the boys a hug and Steele a kiss.

***

Aden answered the phone when Steele called. "Is Dare with you?"

"Yeah, he's here." Aden giggled.

"Did I call at a bad time?" Steele asked, smiling.

"Almost but not quite." Steele heard whispers in the background.

"You're on speaker, and the boys are with us."

Aden cleared his throat.

"Rosa Pena committed suicide today, and Manny escaped and came to kill the boys. He got off two shots, but no one was hurt. One of River's people tried to wing him, but he turned and the bullet went straight to his heart."

"This is Dare. Are the boys okay?"

"Yes. We're going to take them to a child psychologist to make sure of it, but that's not why I called." Steele gave Matteo a hug.

"That's pretty big news. What have you got to top that?" Aden shouted from the background.

"Hector and I are getting married next Monday, and we want the two of you to be our best men."

"Is this already arranged?" Dare laughed.

"No. We figured we'd call your first to see if you

were available on Monday and then call Judge Richardson. We want to get married in his chambers with just the two of you and the boys," Hector told him.

"What about Garcia, Edwards, and White?" Dare asked.

"Yeah, and what about my mom, Sanchez, and Rivers?" Aden added.

"Do you think they'd want to come? We're not planning a party because it's the day before Christmas Eve and the boys just lost their parents. Even though they were what they were, it wouldn't be proper to have a huge celebration outside of Christmas and Christmas Eve for the kids," Steele said seriously.

"Okay, but we get to give you a party after New Year's. Enough time will have passed then that you've given the proper amount of respect to those lowlifes." Dare obviously didn't think they should give them any respect at all.

"If we don't observe the niceties, the boys may feel differently later," Hector added. "As it is, we don't plan on paying for or taking the boys to any funeral."

"Well then, Monday it is. Aden and I will happily serve as your best men. Just call us with the details and we'll be there."

"Good, thank you. I'll call the judge." Hector was about to hang up.

"Hold it. The boys need suits. How about Aden and I take them for suits tomorrow? I'm sure both of you have Christmas things that need to be done."

"You're right. The best things they own are the outfits we bought them for Thanksgiving. For Christmas, we're letting them wear school clothes so they can be comfortable." Steele felt his face redden at a so-obvious omission.

"Aden and I will take them out for suits tomorrow. We'll make a day of it, bonding with our unofficial nephews. We'll pick them up at ten. That gives you a little time to sleep in."

"Not tomorrow. That SOB shot out our kitchen window again. The glazier is coming sometime after eight tomorrow." Hector sighed in resignation.

"We'll come at eight and take them out to breakfast. That way you two can nap on the couch until the glazier arrives. Or do your Christmas chores and, after the glazier is finished, sleep. I know Doctor Huntsman still wants you to rest in the afternoon," Dare chided. "You don't sound like you slept today."

"I didn't with all the excitement. We're at McDonald's, giving the boys unhealthy food for dinner because Rivers chased us out of the house so their CSI team could examine the scene. There wasn't much to examine. Another two bullet holes in the wall. Insurance will pay, but it's still a pain in the ass." Steele's voice sounded gruff even to his own ears.

"What are you eating?" Dare asked with some impatience.

"Don't get huffy. I'm having a garden salad. I know I can't have anything fried." Steele was resigned.

"What kind of dressing?" Dare asked.

"Give me a break, Dare. Oil and vinegar."

"Like I said, I'm a cardiothoracic surgeon. No one of my friends is dying of a heart attack on my watch."

A squeaky voice sounded in the background. "Don't worry, Uncle Dare. Matteo and I are watching

Daddy. We won't let him cheat. We don't want to lose our Daddy."

"Okay, chipmunk, I feel better now that I know you and Matteo are on the job. Uncle Aden has dinner ready. I'm going to go eat. Call us when you have the details."

Hector glanced at the boys. "Does anyone want cookies or ice cream?"

"Cookies," the boys said in unison.

Hector reached into his pocket and handed them a few dollars. "Here, Matteo. Go get you and your brother cookies."

When the boys left, Hector turned to Steele. "Do you have cash on you?"

"Yeah, about a hundred dollars."

"What do you say we give the boys their allowance so they can go Christmas shopping with Dare and Aden? They can take them to Walmart after they buy the suits." Hector chuckled. "The idea of Dare in Walmart makes me laugh. We don't even have to ask them, the kids can."

Steele guffawed, and when the kids came back, they told them the plan.

Saturday Afternoon

"Okay, all of the gifts we purchased are wrapped. Just like I promised, Amazon delivered in two days. Everything is done but the tree, and Sanchez and Rivers are coming tomorrow to help us load it onto the Navigator and into the house. What's next?" Hector gazed at his partner expectantly.

"Well, I was cleared yesterday. We could go into the bedroom and do the deed." Steele leered at

Hector.

"Only if you take it easy."

"I promise not to pound you into the mattress." Steele held his hand to his heart. "Scout's honor."

"You were a Boy Scout?" Hector asked, trying to picture Steele in his scout uniform. "Do you have pictures? I want to see that."

"They threw out all the pictures when they got rid of me."

"Maybe you should call them now that we have the boys. They may have mellowed," Hector suggested. "After all, it couldn't get any worse."

"Maybe I'll call them for Christmas."

"Sounds like a plan."

Hector grabbed Steele's hand and dragged him into the bedroom. "I'm going to prepare myself. You get to watch. I want to watch you touch yourself." Hector undressed and watched him strip. Steele sat on the bed and began to slowly stroke himself.

After Hector finished preparing himself, he pulled Steele underneath him. "I'm going to do all the work. You just lie there with a stiff rod. I'm going to lower myself onto your cock and have you take me slowly."

Hector kissed him, licking his lips and wrapping his tongue around Steele's, taking it into his mouth to suck. He worked his way down his collarbone, biting and kissing. Hector pulled up Steele's arm and kissed the indentation behind his elbow. It was one of his hot spots.

Steele groaned and attempted to grab him. "Not yet. I'm not done."

Hector took both of his hands and squeezed Steele's nubs with his fingers. Steele gasped. Hector put his face on his chest and laved and bit them. He worked his way down to Steele's cock and took it in his mouth, taking it all the way down his throat and massaging it with his throat muscles.

Steele moaned. "If you don't stop that, I'll come before I get inside you, and I desperately want to feel you around me."

Hector got up on his knees and greased Steele's big shaft with lube. He slowly lowered himself. With infinite care, he pushed Steele in and out of his hole until Steel moaned loudly. When Hector thought he was ready, he moved faster until Steele said, "I'm going to blow."

Using his knees as a lever to keep up the movement, he began to stroke his own dick. Steele's face contorted with pleasure as he came. Hector gave himself two more strokes then followed his lover into bliss.

Steele closed his eyes while Hector got the basin and cloth to clean them up. He came back, and Steele was asleep. Gently, he cleaned his lover's chest and genitals then covered him with the sheet and comforter. Hector got dressed, and, after checking on Steele to make sure he was breathing normally, he went into the great room to wrap Steele's Christmas presents.

Chapter Twenty

Monday before Christmas

Hector and Steele went Monday morning and got their marriage license. They, Aden, Dare, and the boys gathered in the judge's chambers for the brief ceremony Monday afternoon. The boys were dressed in their new suits, and they had rose boutonnieres in their lapels with a sprig of evergreen that matched those of their dads'. Aden and Dare sported mistletoe.

The ceremony was solemn despite the fact that it was small. Hector and Steele chose the traditional vows and recited them before the judge who soon pronounced them spouses.

Although they had told Aden and Dare not to fuss, they insisted on taking them out to dinner at Seasons in Albuquerque. The boys were in awe of the napkins, snowy-white tablecloths, and abundance of different spoons and forks. Aden and Dare had the duck, Hector the lamb shank, and Steele had sea scallops. The boys shared the rotisserie half-chicken. Matteo and Felipe had recently learned their table manners from Hector and Steele and performed flawlessly. Aden and Dare took the boys for the evening.

The newly married couple wound up falling asleep on each other on the couch, dressed in their robes and slippers.

Late Tuesday Afternoon

Sanchez and Rivers arrived at four as promised. They brought ropes and bungee cords to tie down the tree. Felipe was jumping around like he had a bedspring attached to his bottom. Hector had gone out earlier that morning and bought still more tree lights. They were ready.

The chipmunk pulled on Hector's belt. "Papa, do we get to ride with you and Daddy?"

"Are you part of this family?" Steele asked.

Felipe hesitated. "I think so."

Hector leaned over and gave him a hug. "I know so. Of course you and Matteo will ride with us. Uncle Jerry and Uncle Jon are taking Uncle Jon's Explorer."

"Matteo, could you please take Felipe's booster seat out of my Explorer and put it in the Navigator. We're taking the Navigator to Jeff's Christmas Trees on Paseo del Norte. Uncle Jon and Uncle Jerry are going to follow us. We're going to buy a huge Christmas tree."

As soon as they got to the lot and Steele stopped the car, the kids wanted out. "Can we go look at all the trees, Papa, Dad?"

"Stay together and don't roam too far away from us. Look for a tall tree that's full so Santa has lots of room to put presents underneath."

It didn't take five minutes for them to spot *the* tree. "Papa, Daddy," the boys shouted as they came running. "Look at this one."

Hector and Steele walked to where the boys were standing. Rivers and Sanchez followed. Sanchez walked around the tree, considering, "That one is a Colorado Blue Spruce. It's nice and tight, so it's fresh, and I don't see any bare spots."

River lifted his head skyward. "It's about twelve and a half feet. Are you sure you want one that big? It's going to be expensive."

Hector gave a side long glance at Steele, who nodded. He went to the proprietor. "How much for the blue spruce, the twelve and a half foot over there where my boys are standing?"

"Two hundred dollars. We'll tie it on top of your car for that price and throw in a tree stand that will fit a tree that big," the man told him.

Steele walked over at the tail end of the conversation, leaving the boys with Jon and Jerry.

"He says two hundred."

Steele nodded. "They're in love with that tree. They haven't looked at another since we got to the lot although Jon and Jerry have attempted to divert their attention."

Hector met Steele's eyes. Steele gave another slight nod. Hector turned to the seller. "We'll take it. It gets tied to the Navigator over there."

The proprietor stared at Hector. "Aren't you Sheriff Gomez?"

"Yes, I'm Sheriff Gomez, Sheriff in Sandoval County...."

"You pulled my kid out of a burning wreck on I-25 this past summer. She got hit by a drunk driver. You got her out just before the car exploded into flames. I always meant to find and thank you for that. I'm Jeff Cobb. You can have that tree for a hundred bucks. That's my cost. My girl came out of that wreck with a few scrapes and bruises. She was trapped in that car. You got her out. We could have lost her that night." The man shook Hector's hand.

"I can't let you do that, Mr. Cobb. It's against the ethical code of the department. If you like, you can donate through the mail to the fund in Sandoval County that helps law enforcement officials who are hurt in the line of duty and their families," Hector told the man.

"Okay, I'll do that." He gestured to two young men who looked remarkably like him.

"Jack, Patrick, help Sheriff Gomez get that twelve-foot blue spruce his kids are standing by over there tied onto the top of that Navigator." Hector took out his card.

Hector had Mr. Cobb run his American Express Card, and the *perfect* Christmas tree was loaded onto the top of the Navigator to head home. Steele and Hector smiled at each other as their chipmunk chattered in excitement.

"Matteo, we have a Christmas tree, a big Christmas tree, and Daddy and Papa said we'd put it and the lights up tonight. We ate turkey. We made Santa cookies. We're going to have a tree, and Santa is coming. Papa, I love you, and I love you, too, Daddy."

"Me, too," Matteo said quietly. "Thank you for taking us."

Hector grabbed Steele's hand and squeezed.

Thursday, Christmas Eve

After eating a stuffed pork roast at Debra's at three, by five everyone was ready to go to Hector and Steele's to decorate the tree with the boys—and to help bring the presents into the house once the boys went to bed. Aden and Dare brought appetizers and canapés. Debra brought homemade biscotti and rum cake, and Jerry and Jon brought eggnog and set up two bowls, one of which had cognac and rum, the other plain. They didn't forget Steele. A carton of fresh apple cider with cinnamon sticks was brought to be heated and served to him and to the kids if they didn't like the eggnog.

The boys admired Steele's Christmas decorations. "These are glass, Dad?" the boys asked of an ornament that resembled a bird with the brushed tail.

"Yes, they're very old. They belonged to my grandmother."

"I'll be really careful, Dad." Matteo gingerly put the ornament on the tree

Hector had the star for the top, and they lifted Felipe onto the ladder to put up the star. He was so excited. "I can put the star on top. Did you hear what Papa said, Matteo? I get to put on the star, and you get to drape the ribbons and bows."

Aden pulled over both boys to see what Hector was doing. "See Papa? He's taking the ribbon and attaching it to the ceiling with the replica of the bird holding the ribbon in his beak."

"What kind of bird is that, Papa?" Matteo stared at the bird Hector was attaching to the ceiling with the ribbon.

"It's a cardinal. It's not a bird native to New

Mexico, but the red color of the bird reminds me of Christmas, so I bought it to carry the ribbon." Hector pushed a few thumb tacks into the ceiling to hold the bird and the ribbon. "Every year I use different ribbon on the tree, and the old ribbon from the year before will help wrap the presents I give to Dad, your uncles, Grandma, and my brothers and sisters and their kids."

Felipe pulled on his belt. "Will Matteo and I get to meet your brothers and sisters?"

"I think I have to tell them that I married Dad first. We're going to see my parents the day after Christmas."

"Does that mean we have another Grandma, a Grandpa, aunts, more uncles, and cousins?" Matteo asked, his eyes big.

"Yes, but I don't know how often we'll see them." Hector grimaced.

"Why, Papa?"

"Because my brothers and my father don't like that I'm gay. My sisters and my mother don't mind, but my father and brothers are difficult about it. They didn't throw me out or anything bad like that, but they do make remarks." Hector told the truth.

"Will my being gay hurt you?" Matteo stood in front of Hector with the last ornament, the one he picked out at the Christmas shop, in his hand.

"No, son. Any hurting is already done, and they have begrudgingly accepted me." Hector sighed. He had been hoping not to have to have this conversation until he spoke to his mamí.

Felipe pulled on his belt again. "What's begrudgingly?"

"That means they didn't want to but did it anyway because Papa is their son," Steele answered.

"So that means they love you even though you're gay?" Matteo was lost in thought.

"That's right. Some people accept you even if they don't like that you're gay." Hector lifted Matteo up onto his lap.

"Yes, sometimes family and friends don't realize or believe that you are born gay and have no choice about it. Everyone here tonight is gay except Grandma and Felipe," Aden said as he passed around the canapés.

"So, people don't know any better and need to be told that you didn't choose it?" Matteo's face scrunched up. "What if they're told and they don't believe it?"

"Then they're ignorant or bigoted, and neither one is a good thing to be." Hector hugged Matteo.

"Where do you want to hang your ornament?" Steele asked.

"Can I hang mine next to yours, Dad?"

"Of course." Matteo hung the little Santa with the lit-up nose. "That's in the right place. See, it was a bare spot," Steele added. "Now it's eight, and that means there are two boys who have to go take their showers, put on their pajamas, and go to bed so that Santa comes. Felipe, go get Santa a plate of Grandma's cookies. Matteo, leave him a cup of eggnog. We'll put a little nutmeg on top."

"Dad, the one with the alcohol or the one without?" Matteo asked, a twinkle in his eye.

"With." Steele winked. "The rum and cognac will warm him up after his long cold sleigh ride. Get a carrot from the vegetable drawer for Rudolph."

"What about the other reindeer?" Felipe wiggled on Steele's lap. "Won't they get mad if Rudolph gets a carrot and they don't?"

"No, chipmunk. We're leaving one for Rudolph because he will guide Santa so he doesn't miss our house. The other reindeer will get carrots from other little boys and girls. Remember, if Santa sees you, he'll leave. So, you have to stay in your room, even if you hear him," Steele said.

"Now, both of you boys go upstairs, take your showers, and get into your pajamas and into bed. Give kisses to your uncles and grandma. Dad and I will come up and kiss you good night." Hector took Felipe off of his lap and dropped him at the bottom of the stairs.

Fifteen minutes later, Matteo called downstairs. "Papa, Dad, we're ready to sleep."

Hector and Steele went up the stairs and gave both boys cuddles and kisses. When they stopped at Felipe's room, their chipmunk was chattering. "Are you sure that he got the address card from Uncle Jerry, Papa? He knows where we are?"

"Yes, he does," Hector assured him.

"Matteo, too?"

"Matteo, too."

The two new dads gave out Christmas kisses and came downstairs to start—with the help of Grandma, Aden, Dare, Uncle Jerry, and Uncle Jon the local equivalent of Santa's elves—loading the piles of Christmas presents under the tree.

"I think that's the last of it, except the bikes. Jon and I will bring those inside. I noticed you didn't have bows for the bikes, so I bought two."

"Thanks, Jerry, Jon, Aden, Dare, Debra. We wouldn't have been able to pull this off without you," Steele said.

The guys and Debra went for their coats.

"I'll be here at ten to help cook," Debra said as

she put on her coat. "Roast prime rib, mashed potatoes, gravy, and some sides. I made another rum cake for dessert. It's a good thing I made two. All of you men devoured the first one."

"Thank you, Debra. We'll see you at ten. I'll have coffee ready at six because I know I won't be able to hold the boys back much longer than that." Steele laughed.

"We'll set up the trains when we get here at noon as soon as they open the packages. We have tracks, an engine, a caboose, a bridge, and a railroad crossing for the matchbox cars." Aden smiled wickedly. "I can't wait to see their faces. Take plenty of pictures. I want to see them as soon as we get here."

"Come on, short stuff. Steele needs his rest, and it's already ten." Dare put his arm around Aden's shoulder.

Aden punched him in the arm. "Keep up with the short jokes and you'll be sleeping in the garage."

Steele and Hector closed the door after their guests left and went into their now bare bedroom. "It's nice to be able to actually walk around the bedroom again." Steele grabbed Hector and tumbled him back onto the bed. "Merry Christmas, baby. Let's make love."

"Only if it's a low-intensity fuck, *mi corazón....* You've been pretty active today."

Chapter Twenty-One

Hector and Steele's Bedroom

"Strip, baby, I want to see you." Steele grabbed Hector around his waist from behind. Hector unfastened his sneakers and toed them off, pulling off his socks and unbuckling his belt. Steele unfastened Hector's belt, pulled his pants and briefs off, and pooled them on the floor. He unbuttoned Hector's shirt, slipped it off his shoulders then put his hand under his T-shirt and pulled it over his head. He made fast work of his own clothing and turned down the covers. Both men got into bed.

Turning, he reached into the nightstand and grabbed the lube, sticking it under his pillow. Steele began to kiss Hector's neck and shoulders and the line of his spine. "Turn over," Steele said in a gruff voice. "I want to taste you."

Steele ran his tongue under the cheek of Hector's ass and up his groin and down the other side. He took Hector's balls in his mouth one at a time and sucked gently.

Hector's shaft was hard and leaking. Steele laid

his head on his stomach and began to lick the pre-cum from his slit. He took Hector's shaft into his mouth and ran his tongue around the head then took Hector down his throat and pursed his lips to increase the suction.

Hector took his fingers and tried to grab Steele's hair for purchase. Steele looked up at him and smiled. "I love you, you self-satisfied bastard."

Hector caressed Steele's head from Hector's cock. "I love you, too. I never expected to fall so hard."

"Neither did I," Steele whispered. "I thought love had passed me by, and then I found you, and you found our boys. Even if I have another heart attack, I'll die happy after having known the love that you and the boys give to me. Turn on your side and let me prepare you."

Steele poured some lube on his finger. He parted Hector's cheeks and ran his finger across Hector's perineum. He ran his finger around Hector's hole and pushed in some lube. He took his time preparing Hector, teasing his hole, kissing and kneading his cheeks. He planted a kiss at the base of Hector's spine, tracing his tongue back down his crack. Biting one of Hector's cheeks lightly, he poured more lube on two fingers and began to stretch his sphincter farther. Hector's whole body relaxed.

Christmas Morning

Hector and Steele awoke to whispers on the stairs. Steele looked at the clock. "Matteo, can't we go downstairs yet? I want to make sure he came, that he didn't forget."

"Don't worry, he came. We have to let Dad sleep. Uncle Dare said he was supposed to rest, and he didn't take his nap yesterday."

The two new fathers threw on their sweats and opened the bedroom door, not forgetting the camera. Hector startled the boys. "I thought I heard little voices on the stairs. Dad is brushing his teeth then we'll go and see what Santa brought. You have to let me go in first so I can take pictures of our first Christmas together."

Steele came out of the bedroom. "Okay, who wants to see what Santa brought?"

Felipe jumped up and down. "All I asked for was a lightsaber. Do you think he had enough?"

"I'm sure of it," Steele said.

Hector stood by the sectional. "Okay, the boys can come in now."

"Oh, Matteo, look, bikes. We have bikes to ride. Santa got us bikes." Felipe was jumping up and down so hard the tree shook.

"Easy, chipmunk. Why don't you and Matteo sort through the presents and make a pile for each of us, and everyone can open theirs together. I'll go and make some hot cocoa with marshmallows and whipped cream and some hot cider for me and—"

Hector interrupted Steele. "I'll have the cider, too. We don't need two of us with clogged arteries."

"So true...." Steele went into the kitchen, watching the boys from over the counter. Their eyes were as big as baseballs when they saw all the packages with their names on them. Although Steele could tell they were dying to tear into them, they waited for him and the cocoa with cookies.

Steele came back with a tray and said, "Let the opening begin...."

Matteo opened one package. "A new computer."

Felipe squealed, "My lightsaber... Matchbox cars with a racing track, *Star Wars* action figures... A computer for me, too, and headphones, a Kindle. Santa must have cleaned out his workshop."

Matteo said in awe, "The Millennium Falcon and an R2D2 that takes commands, a skateboard, oh...a baseball mitt, bat, and baseball. Look, Felipe, a football and a basketball."

Matteo ran to Steele who watched Hector take the pictures. "Thank you, Dad. He finally had a Christmas." Matteo was crying uncontrollably.

"Come on up here next to me, son. Both of you deserved one. Santa thought so, and so did we." Steele surreptitiously wiped under his eye.

"Matteo, I got skates and a basketball and a hoop." Felipe announced every gift.

"Matteo, go open your things," Hector encouraged.

"Can I just watch Felipe for a little while? I want to remember this forever."

"Felipe, we haven't given Papa and Dad their presents."

Felipe put his hand over his mouth. "I forgot."

Matteo went to a small stack of presents. One of them was wrapped very well and looked suspiciously like some others under the tree. "This is for you, Dad, from Papa, Felipe, and me."

Steele opened the square package. Inside was a five-by-seven picture of the two boys with Hector. "It's to put on your desk at work, Dad," Matteo told him. "Papa said that way you can see us all day long and know we're a family."

"Come here." Steele gestured to Matteo, Felipe, and Hector. "I have the best family in the world."

"We love you, Dad," the chipmunk squeaked as Steele gave him a hard hug. "Santa didn't have to bring us so much stuff. I love my presents, but do you think maybe he forgot someone else?"

Steele almost burst into tears. "Papa took some toys to the Toys for Tots program, so we could help to make sure no one was forgotten."

The doorbell rang, and Grandma arrived with all of their uncles. At Uncle Jerry and Uncle Jon's house, Santa left magic tricks for Matteo and a stuffed Mickey Mouse for Felipe, and telephones for both of them. At Grandma's, he left new pants, a coat, shirts, jeans, underwear, and socks. At Uncle Aden and Uncle Dare's house, he left a set of trains to go around the bottom of the tree, an engine, freight cars, and a caboose.

After all the opening was done, Matteo went to sit by Steele. "Dad, is it bad that I don't feel bad that they're dead? I'm sad that they died, but in a way, I'm glad, too, because that means we can stay here and never have to go back. Do you think I'm a bad boy?"

"No, Matteo, not a bad boy, just an honest one."

Hector put some Christmas carols on the new iPod with a docking station that Santa left him under the tree. The boys had one last gift for everyone.

Matteo said, "We didn't have that much money, but we pooled it and got everyone a gift."

Felipe handed Grandma handkerchiefs, their uncles all got key chains with the Lobo's logo, and Dad and Papa received Denver Broncos caps.

Grandma said, "I think I know two boys whose family loves them very much."

Felipe ran to Debra and said, "That's us, Matteo, and we love our family."

In the corner of the room, Steele took a quiet

moment and gave Hector a firm hug and a passionate kiss. "Thank you for loving me, baby."

"You and our boys are easy to love."

About the Author

AC Katt was born in New York City's Greenwich Village. She remembers sitting at the fountain in Washington Square Park listening to folk music while they passed the hat. At nine, her parents dragged her to New Jersey where she grew up, married and raised four children and became a voracious reader of romantic fiction. At one time, she owned over two thousand novels until she and her husband took themselves and the cat to New Mexico for their health and its great beauty. Now, most of AC's books are electronic (although she still keeps six bookcases of hardcovers), so she never has to give away another book.

She hangs out at ACKatt.com; or ackattsjournal.com. She is a very opinionated kitty and at ackatt.com where you may find snippets of her current releases, as well as some from works in progress. She also puts out a newsletter once a month. You can sign up at ackatt@ackatt.com.